I0684544

Blood
of
Huitzilopochtli

A Mario Martinez Mystery

Book Two of the Aztec Series

By Annette Shelley

ISBN 13: 978-0-9841325-2-2
ISBN 10: 0-9841325-2-X

www.annetteshelley.com

Dedication
To Dad

Acknowledgements
To my friends and supporters: Mom, Dad and Mark
Pat Moon, Paula Wagner, Kym Roberts, Cindy Kennedy, and Geri Srikanth
Special thanks to the late Joe Crosson who was with me when I first "met" Mario Martinez nearly ten years ago and encouraged me to pursue and finish this.

Spanish Phrases Glossary

Dear Readers,

I used a few simple Spanish phrases in the book and include this brief glossary here for your reference. Enjoy!

Annette

Amigo - friend
Andale - hurry
Aqui – here
Attencion – attention
Aztecas - Aztecs
Bella – beautiful
Bueno - good
Buenos Dias - good day
Buenos noches – good evening/night
Calle - street
Churros – cookies with cinnamon and sugar on top
Cinco - five
Cincuenta - fifty
Comprende – understand
Cuanto – how much?
Dias – day
El – masculine form of the
Es - is
Flan – Mexican pastry
Hasta manana – until tomorrow
Hola – hello
Huitzilopochtli – Aztec god of war and sacrifice
La – feminine form of the
Magnifico - magnificent
Manana – tomorrow
Mayor – main, primary, major
Menudo – stew made from tripe

Mi – my
Muertos - the dead
Museo - museum
Nada – nothing
Noche - night
Noche Triste – Night of Sorrows
Nombre - name
Numero - number
Palacia – palace
Partido – Political party
Peso – Mexican penny
Policia - police
Por favor – if you please, please
Presidente – President
Problemo – problem
Pulque – hallucinogenic mixture made from cactus pulp
Que - what
Quiere - want
Quetzalcoatl – Aztec Feathered Serpent god
Rapido – quick, fast
Salas – floors or levels in a building
Senor – sir
Senora – ma'am, married woman
Senorita – young woman, unmarried
Si- yes
Stupido - stupid
Tamales – beef rolled in a tortilla and fried
Te - you
Templo - temple
Touristas - tourists
Tres – three
Triste - sad
Uno - one
Y – and
Yo no se – I don't know
Zocalo – city center of Mexico City

DAY ONE

One

Mario Martinez ran up the stone steps of Cathedral Metropolitano toward the bloody altar boy.

"Help! Please somebody help!"

Mario grabbed him by the shoulders. "Are you okay? What is it?"

Nearly out of breath, the little boy cried, "Father Salazar. They've taken Father Salazar."

"Who?"

"The masked men."

Mario's blood ran cold. *Will this nightmare ever end?* "Where? Show me."

The boy who led him inside the Cathedral, past long aisles of gold plated icons of the savior and Mother Mary and confessional booths to the back of the sanctuary. "That way." He pointed to a slightly ajar side door.

"Stay down and don't move." Mario pulled his gun and crept toward the door. He kicked it open and leapt into the side alley, but found nothing but a dried up pool of blood probably belonging to the two Presidential Guards who were killed here the other day.

He went back inside the Cathedral and walked up to the little boy. "Are you sure you're not hurt?"

"I'm okay."

Mario knelt down, looked into the little boy's eyes. "This is where they took Father Salazar?"

"*Si.*"

"You're sure?"

He nodded.

"What did they look like?"

"Big with scary masks on."

Better than nothing. "Okay. Is your mommy around?"

"I can wait with him until she arrives." A middle aged nun approached. Her habit was stained with blood from a gash in the side of her head.

Mario grabbed her until she was steady. "Are you okay, Sister?"

"Hernandez," she said. "*Si.* I fell against a pew, but I'll be alright."

"I'm Mario Martinez. According to this young man, someone kidnapped Father Salazar and brought him back here and out the alley."

Sister Hernandez clutched her rosary. "Oh no. Dear God, what evils has this night brought us? I will pray for his speedy return."

Mario felt the same. "You have my word I will bring him back safely. Did you see anything, Sister?"

She gripped the cross around her neck. "Nothing."

"Are you sure you're okay? Do you need an ambulance?"

"No." She rubbed the side of her head. "I only hope Father Salazar returns safely."

Mario took a look around the strangely vacant Cathedral. "Where is everyone? I saw several nuns here and an entire choir just a minute ago."

"They ran for their lives when those men broke in. I assume they're all at home."

Why would all the nuns leave already? "But you believe they're okay?"

"I'm certain of it."

e also wondered why the policia were already gone. *Strange.* "Fair enough. I will look into this for you, Sister."

"God bless you. I will see to it that this boy gets home safely to his mother."

Mario realized he needed to get to Bene and tell him what happened, and get some direction as to how to proceed from here. Clearly, Father Salazar was nowhere in sight, and the clock began ticking once again. "Thank you, sister. Goodnight."

Two

The poison from the dart fired at Father Salazar's forehead seeped into the awareness centers of his brain and made him feel woozy. Vaguely aware of several large costumed men who carried him underground someplace, he tried to lift his arm in protest, but felt far too tired.

He tried to recall what just happened. He recited the Lord's Prayer, welcomed everyone from the streets outside into the Cathedral for the services and festival honoring the beloved statue of Virgin de los Remedios. The night was beautiful until a band of feathered club and spear wielding maniacs disrupted his service, and a pain in his forehead sent him toppling forward.

Now his limp body dangled over the shoulder of someone. He had no control whatsoever over himself. Before he lost consciousness completely, Father Salazar asked for God's will to intervene in this situation. If he indeed finished his time on Earth, then so be it. If he proved destined to suffer as his beloved Lord and Savior, then he would willingly accept his fate with grace. His only regret would be his inability to help the others with him. He vaguely recalled their screams and panic and prayed for their wellbeing. Salazar clearly recognized his own mortality. His advancing age would make any rescue attempts difficult at best, even if he were still awake. He had faith someone would tend to the weak and helpless and that God had a plan which may or may not be revealed to him personally. His mind pulled farther away from reality with each passing breath, Father Salazar accepted his fate, whatever that may be, and with that final thought, he drifted far away and out of the world of mortal men.

Three

Television reporter Bella Perez received the call about the shootings at Cathedral Metropolitano before anyone else in the city. Maybe her solid journalism skills had something to do with it, but because she worked for the most notorious gossip show in Mexico, her pushup bras, high heels and micro skirts were more likely the secrets to her success.

With her office situated near the Zocalo, she often scooped her competitors and tonight, based on what she'd heard so far, she stood to make journalism history.

She leapt in the production van with her cameraman and they raced to the far side of the Plaza de la Constitucion. She jumped out the door before the driver came to a complete stop, ran up toward the commotion and began smoothing her hair down before the shoot. "You ready with the camera, Pedro?"

"No, not yet," her assistant replied.

She snapped her long fingers together, checking to make sure her new manicure didn't chip in the process. "Hurry up. There's dead bodies out here. We have to get this shot before someone else does."

"Coming. Just a minute." The burly photographer pulled his hand held camera out of its case, leaned it on his shoulder, while a grip set up a spotlight on Bella's face and plugged in the microphones. Within a minute, the production crew began running tape.

Bella checked her above average looks one last time in the side mirror on the van, and stepped back in front of the rampage, careful not to get her three inch high heels caught in the cobblestone on the street. She stood just left of center of the policia and the two dead bodies, and cleared her throat. "Three, two, one…Good evening, ladies and gentlemen. I'm standing outside El Cathedral Metropolitano, sight of the deadly assault that occurred here less than an hour ago when dozens of people dressed in masks stormed into the Cathedral, disrupting services tonight with an outbreak of violence. At least two are confirmed dead. You can see behind me, policia are tending to the two murder victims now." Bella put her hand on her headpiece for dramatic effect, "Oh. Ladies and gentlemen, breaking news just in. I've just received official word Presidente Benito Juarez was among the victims of tonight's Cathedral Metropolitano massacre. According to sources, he was taken moments ago by ambulance to a nearby hospital. I repeat, the Presidente of Mexico, Benito Juarez, injured tonight in a deadly rampage. Keep your televisions right here for the latest updates. I'll be breaking in throughout the night with more on the story once I know more. For now, I'm Bella Perez reporting."

Bella clicked off her mic, turned to the crew, and fluffed her hair, "How did I look?"

The camera man seemed too busy fumbling around with microphones and cables to notice her but the younger grip got an intoxicated smile on his face. He raised his eyebrows and ran his eyes up and down her slender body. "You look great."

She wasn't sure if the compliment was the same coming from a grip, but she smiled anyway and touched up her lipstick. "Good, then let's get rolling to the hospital. Everyone's going to be racing to get there now, thanks to me."

***

Mario hurried down the steps of Cathedral Metropolitano just in time to see the spotlight from the television cameras shut off and Bella Perez combing her hair and applying a fresh coat of lip-gloss. She started to walk away.

He ran up and tapped her on the arm. "Hey."

She spun around, smiled and batted her eyes. "Yes?"

He kept his eyes locked on hers, rather than allowing them to wander to her plunging neckline. "What do you think you're doing?"

"My job." She flung her hair in his face and turned back to her camera man. "Let's go, Pedro."

"Wait just a minute." Mario ran behind her. "*Deadly rampage?* What kind of lies are you spreading out here, huh? You know innocent people were hurt tonight, and they don't need you—"

"Yes and the people of Mexico City have a right to know the truth. Excuse me."

Mario grabbed her arm. "Maybe, but who said you were giving them the truth? Bella, you don't even know the facts. Let me give you the proper information once I get it, okay?"

"Who are you?" She twisted from his grasp and brush herself off. "Let go of me. You're messing up my dress."

The thick necked Pedro sat his camera down, walked over and loomed above the six foot two Martinez. "Hey you. Leave her alone." Pedro's fist was about the size of Mario's head.

Mario held his hands up, took a few steps back and stepped away. "Hey man, sorry. I want to spread the truth, that's all, and I don't think televising this right here and now is serving anyone's best interests. There's a real story here, and you don't have it."

Bella applied a fresh coat of powder on her nose and straightened her sleeves. "I remember you. You're the guy who ignored me when I tried to ask about the kid who got stabbed the other night. So you ready to tell me the big scoop?"

"No, forget it. I have things to do, besides, I don't think you'd know truth if it slapped you in the face. You'd probably twist my words around, make things worse." Mario turned his back on her and walked away.

"Hey wait." Bella ran after him."What's your name?"

"Mario Martinez."

"Were you a witness?"

"Maybe."

"How can I reach you if I have questions?"

Mario kept walking and pulled out his cell to call and check on Bene. "You can't. You had your chance."

Bella ran to catch up to him, her cleavage jiggling, waving one of her business cards in her hand. "Take this, Mario. Please call me first if you get any truthful information, okay?" She batted his eyes at him again.

"Yeah okay." He didn't know why he told her that. He didn't want to call her or anyone else until everyone was safe.   He watched her go, wondering how in the world she managed to run so fast in heels so tall and a skirt so tight. His cell rang over a dozen times now. He nearly pressed end when someone finally answered. "*Senor* Juarez?" Mario asked.

"*Si.*"

"How's Bene?"

"He's in a room for observation, but they say he's going to be just fine thanks to you."

"Senor, I need to come see the two of you tonight.   I'm afraid something else happened right after you left."

"Oh? What's that?"

"I'm sorry *senor*, but I can't talk about it here. It's urgent."

Juarez cleared his throat. "We'll be waiting for you. Meet our people at the back entrance to Juarez Hospital."

"I'm on my way."

Four

When Mario arrived to the Juarez Hospital, dozens of the Presidential Elite Guards flanked the sidewalk outside near the rear entrance. He presented his identification and received an escort up to Bene's room.

Presidente Benito Juarez, the youngest Presidente in Mexican history, lay in a bed and sipped a cold drink while IV fluids helped him catch up from all the other nutrition he missed out on the past few days during his captivity. "Mario." Normally strong and well groomed, Benito had a scraggly unshaven beard, dark circles under his eyes and sullen cheeks.

Mario never felt more relieved to see anyone. "Benito. I am so happy you are okay. And I see they scrubbed the blue paint off of you. That's good."

"I would not be alive tonight if not for Mario, Papa," Bene told his father. "Mario shot the man who nearly carved my heart out of my chest and then he downed all the others before they could put an end to me. You are a true hero. A friend for life. I'm so grateful…" Bene stopped his praise studied his new friend. "Mario? What's wrong? I thought we should be celebrating by now."

Juarez Senior cleared his throat. "Son, Mario has some news you need to hear."

Bene's smile quickly faded. "What is it, por favor?"

Mario hardly knew where to begin. If the events of earlier this evening hadn't been bad enough, more happened. "I hate to be the one to tell you both because I know how close you are to him, but—"

"Get on with it, Martinez." Juarez Senior snapped.

"Father. Give him a minute." Bene lifted his bruised arm to silence his father. "What is it?"

Mario cleared his throat. "After the ambulance took you away, I found out they have Salazar."

"You mean Father Salazar? What, they kidnapped him too?"

Mario hoped this news wouldn't set Benito back on his recovery, but he had to know. "Si, it's true. The same group who terrorized you, killed your friends and my sister now have Father Salazar."

"Did you go after him?" Juarez Senior asked.

"Si, *senor*, I did. After the ambulance came for Benito, one of the young choir boys ran out and told me about it. The poor kid was covered in blood. He showed me where he last saw Salazar and he took me out the back of the Cathedral, but Salazar was nowhere in sight. The door was open and when I went to see where it led, it opened into the side alley."

Bene choked up, his eyes misted with tears. "That's the same place where I saw Diego and Jorge…Sorry. It's still hard for me to believe my two best friends are dead."

"What about Ricardo?" Juarez Senior asked Bene. "Did he help you while you were being held captive?"

Bene got quite emotional. "No, I…don't know how to tell you this, but he is the one who kidnapped me. He killed Jorge and Diego with his bare hands and took me out to the middle of nowhere."

"What? I can't believe it." Juarez Senior said. "Is he still alive?"

Bene rolled his head on his pillow. "*Yo no se*. He may be, I'm not sure."

"I doubt it," Mario said. "I went out to the temple earlier today where I think you were being held, Bene. I saw an awful lot of blood inside that place. I've got a strange feeling some of it might have belonged to Ricardo. We will need to get expert forensic people in there to investigate tomorrow to make sure."

Bene leaned his head deeper into his pillow and cleared his throat to choke back the tears. "Si."

Mario felt terrible for poor Bene. He'd lost everything that ever meant anything to him. "Don't get worked up, Bene. You need to rest, get well."

Bene blinked acknowledgement, but was too torn up to speak at the moment.

"So what do we know about these people?" Juarez asked Mario.

"From what I learned, they are obsessed with the Ancient Aztec culture and may believe they are the gods themselves. That maniac who tried to kill Bene had a ceremonial mask on, and the others were dressed in feathers, beads and costumes reminiscent of the old Aztec customs. The policia will have to investigate more of this tomorrow, but the thing is, there is no telling with these people. They are insidious. When I went to untie you

Bene, they all disappeared and since most wore masks, there will be no way to catch any of them."

Juarez Senior patted Mario on the back. "Si, but you did catch the man who personally tortured my son and for that, we are grateful. I'll never be able to repay you, Martinez."

Mario didn't feel comfortable receiving accolades. He hadn't done anything exceptional in his mind. "But this isn't over yet. Even if Father Salazar hadn't been kidnapped, these people are extremely dangerous. We discovered Pena, but even though he's out of the way now, somebody took Father Salazar, so this organization must run deeper than we think. From what I could tell, these people truly believe Bene is one of the old Aztec gods, and that is why they wanted to kill him."

Juarez senior laughed. "How could that be?"

"For some reason, they see Bene as *Quetzalcoatl*, the Feathered Serpent, because of his beard, his paler skin, the way he rose to power and essentially came out of nowhere in their eyes."

"That's preposterous. Ridiculous." Juarez Senior laughed.

"You don't need to take my word for it, Senor Juarez," Mario said. "But I've talked extensively with people who validate this theory and I think it's something to consider for future. With Father Salazar now missing, we need to be aware that even though the main figurehead and a few others were killed earlier tonight, we are dealing with very sick people here who have some delusional vision of reality, and from what I can tell, there might be hundreds of them."

"He's right. They were everywhere. Hundreds, maybe thousands. This isn't something that's going to stop overnight." Benito got a faraway look on his face. "I still can't believe our family friend Judge Pena tried to kill me. He seemed like such a nice man, but to think…" He choked back tears. "Pena must have gone mad from drinking too much pulque."

"There's no telling what went wrong, but there is no excuse for what that man almost did to you and my sister. I'm just happy you're safe and…" Mario's eyes misted and he had trouble continuing.

"What?"

"I found Angela's body, and all I know is how glad my mother will be, especially since I promised her I would find Angela and bring her home."

"They found her?" Bene asked. "Where?"

"On the steps of the Cathedral. They threw her body down the steps tonight along with the cleaning lady from the Musco I told you about. All in line with ancient Aztec custom."

Benito bit his trembling lip. "Oh my God."

Juarez Senior held his son's shoulder. "I'm so sorry, Bene."

"Si, it is horrible, but my mother will…" Mario's heart nearly stopped when he realized he left his mother and Sylvia at the hospital. "Oh no. My mother. Gentlemen, I have to run for tonight and go meet my mother. Tomorrow first thing I will be in your office, Senor Juarez and we will make the plans for recovering Father Salazar."

"That is if he's still alive," Juarez Senior said.

Mario felt optimistic. "There is always hope, Senor. Bene came home to us in one piece, so perhaps Salazar will also be spared."

"Si," Bene said.

"We need a team of men we can trust to help us. I told you before, I cannot do this alone. Are there any men who we can trust with our lives?" Mario asked.

Bene's eyes misted. "To think the three people who I trusted most in this world are now gone and that one of them is responsible for their deaths is unbelievable to me. I don't have to tell you, Mario, how corrupt our government can be, and I am very afraid for all of us because I don't know who I can trust. My father and I will discuss this and we will decide by tomorrow first thing on how to proceed, okay?"

"That's all I can ask. We don't have much time. We must secure the proper people who we know we can entrust with incriminating evidence, and who I can work with to bring these vicious killers to justice."

Juarez Senior extended his hand to Mario. "I will look into this at once, and meanwhile, we are so grateful to you. We need you to head up this investigation and put an end to this as soon as possible."

Mario hoped he could. "Si senor. You have my word I will do my best."

"I will see you manana," Bene smiled.

"No you won't son." his father protested, "You will need to rest."

"Father, how can I rest when my people are under attack from this unseen force? I will never rest again until whoever is responsible for this is either dead or in prison."

For once, Mario agreed. "You need rest, Benito. I will do whatever I can to bring your friend Father Salazar home safely to you. For now, I must go."

***

When Mario got downstairs, he went outside to the front of the hospital to go to the Metro station and laughed when he saw Bella Perez pushing against the policia trying to get inside the hospital.

"Don't you know who I am?" She bent over in front of the policia, seductively flashed a smile and a little skin. "I broke this story, and I deserve to get inside there tonight."

"Senorita, I'm afraid nobody has access to this area. We need to ask you and your crew to back away now, or we'll put you in jail."

Mario couldn't help it, he had to say something. "What's wrong, Bella? Denied access?"

She frowned at him. "What are you doing here?"

"Oh nothing," Mario laughed and went to get on the train.

Five

The Executive sat in his office smoking a cigar, feet kicked up on his coffee table. "Judge Pena told me Mario Martinez would not be a problem, but apparently he was wrong."

His closest advisor sat across from him sipping on tequila. "What do you mean, boss?"

"Pena is dead. He hauled Benito Juarez into the Cathedral and tried to execute him there, out in the open, rather than in the more discreet location we already selected. Now our entire organization is at risk thanks to that idiot, and this Mario Martinez saved the day."

"What do you want me to do, boss?"

The executive took a sip of brandy, stared out his window into the Zocalo where the policia were still busy scouring the crime scene on the Cathedral steps, "I suppose it's time for Plan B."

***

"Good evening. I'm Bella Perez. Still no word on the status of El Presidente Benito Juarez. El Presidente was brought to the hospital behind me less than an hour ago. Sources say Juarez was inside the Cathedral Metropolitano when rapid gunfire erupted and two bodies turned up in the Zocalo earlier tonight. So far, there is no word on his condition, and Presidential spokespeople did not return my phone calls. Rest assured, we will follow this story through the night and will have all the latest at ten. This is Bella Perez reporting." Bella turned off her mic, and ran her hands on her skirt, pulling it tighter over her hips. "Well? How did I look?"

Neither of her crew listened at the moment, so she turned to catch a glimpse of her reflection in the front window of Juarez Hospital. Inside the lobby policia packed into every available space. She wanted in there. She deserved to be in there because the people deserved to know what happened to their Presidente.

She thought about that idiot, Mario Martinez and wondered why he kept showing up everywhere she went. He was kind of cute, sexy even, but he didn't seem to notice her like all the other men she knew. He seemed like a self centered, self serving jerk, but something about him made her wonder. He might have answers to some of her questions. Then again…

"Hey Bella." Pedro said. "Now what?"

"Get your pillow and blanket. We're spending the night right here." Bella sat on the concrete steps and smiled.

Six

B y the time Mario rode the metro to the hospital on the northern side of Mexico City and rode the elevators up to the twelfth floor, his mother was sound asleep in the waiting room, her head pressed against a wall. He quietly walked up to her and tapped her shoulder. "Mama?"

His mother jumped. "Where have you been? I've been worried sick."

"Mama, I found Benito. He is in the hospital and he will be okay," Mario smiled.

His mother's eyes filled with tears. "You think I care about that high and mighty *Presidente* when your sister is dead and missing?"

"Mama—"

Elsa threw up her arms. "No I don't, okay? This is all his fault our Angela is dead, Mario, and I don't care what you say. If I can't even give my baby a proper funeral, then—"

"Mama. Listen. I found Angela today too. She will come home to you."

"Alive? Did someone make a mistake?" His mother threw her arms around him and kissed him a half dozen times.

Mario felt horrible. "No, mama. I meant I found her body, her remains, so we can bury her now."

His mother began her heaving sobs, shrinking into his arms. "Oh—"

"I'm so sorry."

"How will I go on? How can I?"

Mario grabbed her by the shoulders. "You need to pull yourself together and be strong. Do it for Angela, do it for me. We must both go on and find the people who did this to our Angela, Mama, because they are evil and they are spreading this evil around Mexico City. I cannot even tell you all I saw tonight or it would scare you so badly you would never leave your house again."

Sylvia, his mother's next door neighbor, walked up, "Elsa? Mario? Is everything okay?"

"Si, they found Angela's body today," Elsa Martinez cried to her friend.

"Oh no." Sylvia took Elsa's hand.

"How is Carlos? Did he ever wake up?" Mario asked Sylvia.

"Si, he is awake. He was not in a coma like they thought before. Carlos had a very severe reaction to the anesthesia and the…" she broke off in tears, "blood loss…"

The two women consoled each other, while Mario went to find Carlos' room. With any luck, the young boy who witnessed much of the brutality of the last three days would wake up and could give him new detailed information or clues, that might help bring Salazar back home safely. He walked down the long hallway until he ran straight into a nurse's station. Three attractive female nurses were busy sifting through a pile of charts nearly a half a foot thick.

"Hola. I need to find the room for Carlos Ortiz."

A nurse glanced up from her chart. "You family?"

"I am *with* his family," Mario pointed to Sylvia and his mother in the waiting room.

The nurse shrugged. "Down the hall, third door on the left."

"Gracias." Mario followed the directions and found the door marked *Ortiz* on the outside. He tapped lightly on the door. "Carlos?"

Nobody answered.

He opened the door as quietly as he could. The young boy's eyes were closed, he had more tubes running through him than anyone should. A slow beeping noise from a nearby monitor showed signs of distress. Mario hoped Carlos would pull out of this okay. "Carlos?"

Carlos cracked his eyes open. He made a slight noise, but still seemed pretty groggy.

Mario realized Carlos may or may not remember him. Carlos lived next door to his mother, but after losing so much blood, he might not recall falling at his feet after being stabbed in the stomach two nights ago. "I'm Mario Martinez, Elsa's son. I saw you the other night after your...*accident*."

Carlos whispered ever-so-slightly. "*Presidente...*"

Mario smiled. "I found *Presidente* Juarez. He is going to be okay.   He is alive and well tonight, thanks to you."

Carlos seemed both pleased and agitated by this latest news. He fidgeted in the bed, his head rocked back and forth on his pillow and he started to hiccup slightly. Tears formed in his eyes. "I..."

"You didn't do anything wrong, Carlos. You did the right thing coming home and telling us." Mario wanted to add *even if it did nearly cost you your life,* but instead he said, "You were very brave. Now I need more help. Those people you were with the other night are doing very bad things, and it's getting worse. They've..." Mario had to think about whether or not he should tell the kid about Salazar. No. Probably not. Carlos seemed upset enough. "I don't want you to worry about it now, Carlos. Tomorrow when you are feeling better, maybe we can talk about it then, okay?"

"*Si.*"

"I just want to know one thing today, if you can remember. Do you know who brought you into the organization? Who is in charge?"

"No," Carlos whispered.

"You don't know a name?"

Carlos shook his head.

"But someone invited you?"

"*Si.*"

"Do you know what the person looked like?"

Carlos whispered. "Big, giant...tattoos all over...gave me money..."

"Did you happen to catch his name?"

He shook his head and made a slight noise.

"Did you get the name of *anyone* you worked with that day?"

"Ricardo."

Ricardo. Mario knew the name - Bene's murderous childhood friend. "Where is Ricardo? Can you tell me where I can find him?"

Carlos' lip quivered, his eyes filled with tears. "Murdered. Templo." His head fell back on his pillow.

Mario hated to keep pressing, but he needed to know. "You're saying Ricardo was murdered at the Temple the other day?"

"Uh huh."

"You're sure?"

"I...saw." Carlos closed his eyes, and fell back to sleep.

An eye witness. Carlos' stabbing now made a lot more sense. Mario cringed at the thought. He couldn't be in all these places at once. With any kind of luck, the people responsible believed Carlos dead, if not, he would need protection Mario feared he couldn't provide.

DAY TWO
July 2

Seven

First thing the following morning, Mario met with Benito and his father.

Juarez Senior patted him on the back. "Thank you for agreeing to do this for us. We don't know who else to trust. We believe we've screened out some loyal policia to assist, but as you know, we cannot be too certain of anything anymore, based on the past few days."

Frustration mounting, Mario wished he could find someone else to help him. "How will we know these men are trustworthy?"

Benito reclined in the chair behind his desk, his arm in a cast and a few cuts on his face. "Sadly, we won't. My father and I handpicked some of our best men to assist you. This morning, each will have a new cell phone, and unbeknownst to them, these phones are tracked and bugged with feeds coming direct to my office. Rita will keep up with it all."

Juarez Senior paced around the room in his typical style. "I still think it's unrealistic for Rita to do all this, but we have no choice."

"My father and I don't have all the bugs worked out yet, but in my opinion, this is the only way. My best friend turned against me, our personal friend tried to kill me. Clearly, we don't know who the players are in all this yet, and we may never know."

Mario knew he would have to break the news about Ricardo. Poor Benito would be devastated when he found out. "Si, I agree. We must assume we cannot trust anyone until they prove themselves. It's a sad way to operate, but…"

"Necessary," Bene said.

Mario cleared his throat, swallowed hard. *God, I don't want to do this.* "Um…speaking of untrustworthy friends…"

Bene wrinkled his brow. "What?"

"I went to visit the young boy Carlos last night in the hospital."

Juarez Senior leaned forward in his chair. "Did he give any solid information we can use?"

Mario shrugged. "Yes and no. He did tell me a giant man with a tattoo offered him money to join, but he didn't have any names of who was in charge. When I asked him if he happened to catch the names of anyone else in the organization, he mentioned someone by name."

"Who?" Bene asked.

Mario cleared his throat again. "Ricardo."

Once the name fully registered in Bene's mind, the poor man looked ill. "I see…This is what I'm talking about. When I found out I couldn't trust Ricardo, I realized there is nobody I can trust but you, Mario. Family only. My father, Rita and you. That's it."

Mario sighed with relief, lowered his eyes. He didn't have another true friend in the world besides Benito either now that Angela was gone. She always looked out for him before, had his back. "Si, I understand."

Bene leaned back in his chair, knit his fingers together. "You know, Carlos saved my life. Ricardo turned into a madman, nothing like the boy I grew up with my whole life. He probably would have shot me through the head or worse if Carlos hadn't been with him. Carlos opened the trunk and untied my gags. He showed compassion and that's when I realized he was brainwashed."

Mario didn't know about that. He couldn't understand what motivated people to do evil things, he hated the fact Sylvia would be kept wondering who lured her son into the organization. She would surely blame herself for not raising him right. He wished he could find out what really happened. "I'll ask him when…*if* he wakes up."

"We will all pray he does." Juarez Senior put his head in his hand. "I still can't believe you lived through all of this. Thank God!"

Mario still couldn't believe it either. Two more minutes and Benito would have been carved in two. "One more thing, Carlos witnessed Ricardo's murder at the same temple where you were held."

Juarez Senior scowled. "Are you sure?"

Mario shrugged. "I do. Carlos has no reason to lie. Once we find Salazar, we need to get out there and check it out. The site was a bloody mess the other day."

"Do you think they took Salazar there?" Bene asked.

"No. They chose that temple because of a holy event. Now that's over, we need to look at a calendar. I'm going to start researching today to find out what other sacred festivals and events are coming up. They seem to operate on a short time frame and there's a chance if we can figure this out, we can find Salazar alive and well long before it goes as far as what happened at the Cathedral the other night. I have a strange feeling Father Salazar is closer to us now than we realize, so we need to work fast."

"This office will do whatever it can to help you," Benito said.

In the military, Mario trained to remain level headed under time pressure and dire circumstances. He never dreamed he would need these skills so soon though. "I don't know what I've gotten myself into here, but I will see this through to the end, for personal reasons, if nothing else."

"Si, I understand, and believe me, we want you to, but there's only one problem," Bene said. "Where do we begin?"

Mario remembered the last time Benito asked the same question and by the grace of God, things worked out. He never shook the feeling about the restricted area in the Templo Mayor. Someone was hiding something down there. "I need a search warrant as soon as I can get one."

"For what?" Juarez Senior asked.

"There is a locked doorway on the lower level of the Museo near the spot where Rosa was probably taken after she disappeared. Everyone at the Museo are uptight about it and get upset when I ask questions. Director Montoya forbid me to go there under any circumstances. I believe to find Salazar alive, we must get in there this morning."

"What do you think is in there?" Benito asked.

"There are tunnels underground in the city center supposedly built by the Aztecs. I personally believe the door might lead under the ruins and could be serving as access for the killers to move around unnoticed."

"You really think they're keeping Salazar there, right under our noses?" Bene asked.

"It's a hunch, but *si*, I do. I also believe the construction company used by Templo Mayor might be involved. Something's not right. I need that warrant."

"But…" Juarez Senior began.

"Father. I will make this decision. If Mario needs a warrant, I will have one prepared within the hour. Go tell Rita to type it up and round up five of our best policia to go with him."

For once, Juarez Senior backed off. "Si."

Bene turned to Mario. "You'll have full cooperation of the Mexican Government and my office. No matter what the cost, we need to put an end to this immediately. And as far as researching upcoming events, Rita can do that."

"No," Mario interrupted. "She's got enough to do. I'll do it once I get my warrant."

"Let me do some searching," Juarez Senior said. "It'll take my mind off things."

"I can look too," Bene said. At that moment, the phones in the outer office rang off the hook.

Bene and Mario glanced at each other.

Mario shook his head. "You don't have time to help, Bene, neither do you, Senor Juarez."

Benito leaned back in his chair and got a faraway look in his eye. "It's starting already, Amigo. The media caught the disaster in the Cathedral last night on film, and it will only get worse if you don't stop it now."

The pressure to succeed in life never felt greater than at this moment. Mario remembered as a kid how scared he got in school right before a big test. This felt similar, only now the consequences of failure could prove deadly. He must succeed in stopping this organization. Failure wasn't an option. Determination and resolve filled him. "Get me that warrant, Bene, and I will put an end to this once and for all."

Eight

Rita didn't know how to respond to the dozens of phone calls flooding the office regarding El Presidente's trip to the hospital. The reporters behaved rudely, many demanded the exact room he stayed in, names of doctors and nurses who tended him and other personal details. She took all their phone numbers and issued a statement. "El Presidente is fine and he will conduct a press conference later this morning to clear up any misunderstandings."

***

Juarez Senior growled. "A press conference? Today? You're out of your mind, Rita."

"What did you want me to say, Senor Presidente?" Rita turned to Benito for support. "The people demand information about their Presidente."

"You do not call press conferences without asking someone first." Juarez Senior shouted. "It's not your place."

"Father, enough. Rita's right. The people need to know I'm okay. Especially after the bloodbath on the square last night, since it's all over the TV, newspapers and radios, we must respond and put citizen's minds at ease."

"But look at yourself, Bene. Did you take a good look in the mirror? Your head is cut open, your beard is all…oh I don't know." He sighed and threw up his hands. "I can't make these decisions for you, son. Do it yourself."

"I appreciate your advice, father, but I will see the people. Regardless of how I look, it's necessary." In many ways Bene's father still treated him like a little boy rather than the leader of the nation. "Rita, tell everyone the press conference will be held in front of the Palacio at 2:00 p.m. this afternoon."

"*Si, senor*." Rita slipped out of the office before he could change his mind.

Bene stepped to the mirror in the corner of his office to see what his father complained about. True, his left eye was slightly blackened, his cheeks thinner than normal after three days without food. A deep cut lined the center of his forehead. All in all, he looked like hell warmed over. Despite this, another aspect of his appearance bothered him far more. "You're right, dad. I'm a mess."

"Now you're coming to your senses," Juarez said.

"Go get me a razor, will you?"

Juarez Senior appeared a few moments later with the razor, handed it to Bene. "Here you go."

Benito steadied his shaking hand on his elbow and carefully shaved his beard.

Juarez Senior seemed alarmed. "Son, what are you doing?"

"Mario said my beard bothers people."

"What? That's ridiculous!"

Benito ignored him and kept shaving. "I have to get rid of it."

"Haven't you seen enough cutting for a lifetime these past few days?"

Bene tilted his head and lifted his lower lip, running over the area until it felt smooth as silk. "Apparently some people believe I am the returned god Quetzalcoatl."

"Normal people don't. You can't allow crazed maniacs to ruin your appearance, son. Your beard is your brand. It got you elected. What if people don't recognize you anymore?"

Benito would hear nothing of it. "Has Mario been wrong about anything yet?"

"Well, no…"

"And I know with great certainty the people we're dealing with are anything but normal."

"Yes, but…"

Benito put the razor down and glanced at his father. "I can't risk it. I need to… calm them down…something. Make them like me and see me in a more neutral way." He lifted his chin, stroking the blade carefully along the lines of his neck.

Juarez Senior sighed. "That is about the stupidest thing I've ever heard."

"You want people subconsciously associating me with Cortez?"

"No, but you don't cater to these people. You are the leader. You dictate policy."

"I don't care what you think. This topic is not up for debate. Hundreds gathered in that Cathedral last night, all aligned with this terrorist organization. There are probably hundreds more who were not there. Plus, there's no way to know who they are and where to find them, but I promise, they're everywhere. I can feel it. The bottom line is, if my beard bothers them, I must take it off. I can't risk enflaming them anymore. Father Salazar's life depends on it. I must be more likable to the people."

"You are likable to the people who matter."

Bene finished removing the final section and turned to face Juarez Senior. "See? What do you think?"

"You look like you're twelve."

He chuckled. "No I don't. Besides, I have no choice."

"There's always choice."

"No." Bene admired his new profile in the mirror. "There isn't."

Nine

Archbishop Father Salazar lay in a pool of his own blood on a cold stone floor, his hands tied behind his back.

When the faint light of day peeked in the cracks of the stone walls, he opened his eyes, surprised by his poor physical condition and shocked to be alive.

His head felt split open, his body felt broken and bruised. He tried to release his arms which felt pulled from the sockets, but he couldn't. Being in one's eighties left little in the way of excess physical stamina.

Salazar felt certain God would call him home soon. He'd been spared for now because God needed him for something. He hoped his time was short and his pain could end soon. The moment he entertained such selfish thoughts, he felt guilty. His pain couldn't come close to the suffering of Christ. God had a reason for his life. He would continue to serve his fellow man until his final breath and would remain on Earth with grace and dignity until God called him home.

For now, with nothing else to do and no particular direction, he did the only thing he could. He prayed.

***

Two men had a brief mid morning phone conversation on untraceable.

"Martinez went to the hospital late last night."

"Oh?"

"*Si,* he went to see the boy."

Silence on the line, then finally, "Is he is talking yet?"

"I don't know."

"I see…"

"What do you want to do about it?"

"Does the boy know anything?"

"I don't know."

"Well, does he or doesn't he? Yes or no?"

"*Si*, he went to the location, rode with *El Presidente* and met the Judge too. There's no telling."

"Then why do you waste my time calling? You know what I'm going to say."

"Si…"

"Then get it done. Fast. And one more thing."

"Yeah?"

"From now on you don't talk to me anymore."

"But…"

"There's a new leader now. Answer directly to him."

"Who?"

"Don't worry about the particulars. Believe me, he will find you when the time is right. You'll hear from someone within the next twenty four hours. Now take care of the problem and stop bothering me." He hung up the phone.

Ten

M ario couldn't help smiling. He and ten of the Presidente's toughest guards showed up at Templo Mayor that morning with a search warrant for the property. This moment felt too good to ignore. Finally he had access to the one place nobody wanted him to see.

"I will never let you go down there." Dennis Montoya screamed.

Montoya's tirade made the warrant all the more satisfying. Mario needed to know why Montoya got so upset about the door. He was hiding something, for sure.

Just before things went from ugly to terrible, Amelia Sanchez appeared. "What's going on? I heard shouting and…" She turned toward Mario. "Why are you here?"

Mario raised the warrant for everyone to see. "With all due respect, Senora Sanchez, this warrant signed by El Presidente grants me access to search the restricted area downstairs this morning."

Sanchez looked flustered. She waved her hands around, stammered her speech. "Well, you should give us some notice…"

He still believed Sanchez innocent of wrongdoing. "No Senora, we don't. The only notice I'll give you this morning is to terminate my employment at Templo Mayor effective immediately so I can conduct this search. Now I must insist you step back and let us do our job."

"I will not stand for this," Dennis Montoya shouted. "Martinez is a kid. Who does he think he is telling us what to do?" He looked to Sanchez like a child being picked on in school.

Sanchez stood her ground. "No Dennis. Do what they say. Go get the keys and meet us downstairs, *comprende*?" She gave him a knowing glance.

Montoya pouted, mumbled under his breath and wandered off like a hurt puppy.

Mario's smile got a little brighter. "Gracias, Senora. I promise once we take a look, we'll be on our way."

"Why do you insist on pressing? I thought we handled this the other day."

Mario refused to offer excuses or explanations. "*El Presidente, senora.*"

Sanchez sighed. "Some things are better left alone. Your sister was never down there. I promise."

"How do you know?"

She gave him a ruffled look, mumbled something under her breath and stormed down the steps.

Mario turned to the other officers. "I guess the Senora Sanchez hasn't seen the newspapers or the television yet today, or else she might know why we're here."

The men laughed and everyone followed her.

***

Dennis Montoya fumed when he disappeared into the museum office he shared with Senora Sanchez. Luckily Sanchez cleverly gave him the proper excuse he needed to slip away and make a phone call. He hoped it would do some good. He picked up the phone and dialed.

A man answered. "Hola?"

"Si, this is Montoya. There's a little problem…"

"Oh?"

"*Si.* His name is Mario Martinez…"
***

Montoya reappeared a few minutes later, keys in hand.

"What took you so long?' Senora Sanchez asked.

"I couldn't find the keys. Here they are." He held them up and made his way through the policia and Martinez, who waited outside the door of the restricted area.

"Hurry up, Montoya," Martinez said. "We don't have all day.

Montoya wished he could put that smartass out of his misery, but other people were more qualified to tend to such matters. He shuffled through the thirty plus keys on the ring, hoping to waste just enough time so things would work out in their favor.

Sanchez tapped her heels on the floor. "Jerry, this isn't rocket science. Give those to me." She reached out for the key ring.

Montoya held up the key, laughing nervously. "Ah here it is." He slipped it in the lock. The door creaked open.

Eleven

F ather Salazar curled up in a ball on a small cot in a freezing stone room wondering what happened. By some act of good fortune, someone untied his hands. He struggled trying to break free from his other restraints, soon ran out of energy, and tucked his head in his hands, both to pray and to keep his head warm. Finally pure exhaustion consumed him. Sounds of a heavy door slamming outside his cell, heavy footsteps and the sound of a key turning in the lock startled Salazar just before he lost consciousness.

The time of reckoning was here. If God wanted him alive, so be it, if not, he would gladly accept His will. He sucked in his breath and tried to appear calm and dignified when the door opened.

"Hey you." A giant covered in tattoos marched to his cot, shoving him in the arm. "Time to get your Holier-than-thou ass up. We've gotta move."

Salazar rolled to one side in a failed attempt to jump to his feet and avoid further injuries. He fell on the floor and crawled on his knees until he could prop himself up on the cot and silently walked toward the man. In the very deepest parts of his mind, he imagined rushing past him, getting away. He knew of the caverns beneath Cathedral Metropolitano, and although he hadn't wandered here in years, he might find his way out. "Where are we going?"

The giant grabbed his forearm, ushered him toward the door. "We're taking you someplace else."

Salazar realized he should keep quiet, but there was an outside hope if he could talk to this young man, he might persuade him to have mercy. "No need. I am perfectly fine here."

"Shut up old man." The brute slapped him across the face, sending him back to the floor.

The priest quickly lost hope for his escape plans. Thirty years ago maybe, but even then, he never possessed the size or girth of this man. He stayed on the ground until commanded to move.

"Go on. Get up. You're not gonna give me a hard time anymore, are you?"

Salazar stood as quickly as he could. "No."

"Good because I don't want to hurt you. My mom would kill me if I did."

Like most of the people of this community, Salazar realized he probably knew his captor's family. "Oh? Do I know your mother? Is she one of my parishioners?" Salazar found a glimmer of hope.

"None of your business. I don't feel right about doing harm to a man of the cloth."

Salazar clasped his hands in prayer and bowed his head. "I'll do my best to obey."

"Hold out your hands."

Salazar noticed the open door behind him, wishing, hoping.

"I said *hold out your hands*," the giant yelled.

Reluctantly but solemnly, Salazar put both arms straight out in front of him.

The man slapped heavy metal cuffs around his wrists bound together by two heavy black chains, then attached the entire apparatus to his waist.

Sanchez considered loosening his own belt, freeing himself once they were outside, but decided against it. The man stood at least six foot six. His waist reached Salazar's chin.

"Come on. Walk." He shoved Salazar in the back. "Hurry up. We're running out of time."

Salazar wanted to ask why, but valued his ribs. One already felt broken. He stood still, waiting for the man to move.

"Hey, go on. You go first." He shoved Salazar again, causing him to stumble on the stone floor.

Salazar lifted his hands in surrender. "Fine, but I don't know where I'm going."

"Straight ahead. Get outside. I'll show you."

Twelve

Mario rolled his eye, sick and tired of Montoya and his stupid parlor tricks. He thought about kicking the door in himself, but out of respect for Senora Sanchez, he calmed himself.

Montoya finally found the key, opened the door.

He held his breath. He waited felt sure a huge break in the case would come from this.

He peeked inside and his heart sank. The room contained nothing except dozens of large transformer boxes with wires sticking out every which way. He scratched his head. *Was this it? Surely not.* He shined his flashlight, carefully looking everything over. Maybe Montoya and Sanchez told the truth. "What is this, *Senora* Sanchez?"

Sanchez stood with her arms folded. "I told you. It's the transformer boxes, the electrical circuit boards which run the power to this entire complex. There is nothing back here."

He respected her opinion, but stepped inside anyway, pushing the wires out of the way, slowly working his way toward the back of what appeared to be nothing more than a dusty supply closet. "Let me check this, *senora.* I need to give a report to *El Presidente*."

Sanchez stood directly behind him, arms crossed. "Fine."

Disappointed his hunch turned out to be nothing, Mario worked his way through the disorganized tangle of wire, unable to shake the fact Rosa vanished into thin air. There was no other way out besides this closet. She had to have come through here. He knew it, but now, he knew realized it would be hard to squeeze a body, even one as slight as Rosa's, through such a mess. He almost gave up and turned around, when h pulled more wires back and found a huge black cloth hanging floor to ceiling.

"You satisfied now?" Montoya sneered.

Ignoring them both, Mario reached out and to his stunned amazement, found the cloth moved freely and blocked an opening. "Wait, I think I found something." He reached behind the remaining wires, pulled the cloth back, exposing a stone cavern.

Senora Sanchez gasped. "Oh my God."

Mario shined his flashlight into the tunnel and signaled for the others to follow. "Come on, fellas. We found what we came here for."

They walked through the opening, single file, each man doubled over to squeeze through the low lying rooftop for the first several feet. Then the tunnel opened up so they could stand fully upright. Incredibly, Mario's light ran out before the tunnel did. "This goes way back here, I'm guessing at least a quarter of a mile or more."

"Where does this lead?" one of the officers asked him after they walked quite a ways inside.

He shined the flashlight up, down and all around the cave made of ancient stones probably left behind by the Aztecs themselves. He led the entourage deeper into the tunnel. "I don't know for sure where it goes. If I did, I wouldn't need a search warrant, now would I?"

The space narrowed again the further back they went. They doubled over and squeezed through. Although he would never admit it aloud, Mario hated cramped spaces and felt a little queasy. He hoped they would find the end soon.

At least ten more minutes passed while they slowly crawled through the tight space until the ceiling opened up. About the time they could all stand up straight again, they ran into a solid stone wall with a door in the middle.

"Damn it." Mario pounded his hands against a thick wooden door with dark metal hinges and a padlock. "Break the door down." He stepped aside while two officers pulled nightsticks from their belts.

Sanchez clicked up to the door in her heels. "Excuse me, but this is a historical site. You can't do that."

He spun around. "Look, *senora*. The rules changed once they kidnapped El Presidente and murdered innocent people. We will do whatever necessary to find out what's hidden behind these walls." He turned to the officers. "Get ready, gentlemen. We're going inside, one way or another."

The officers all stepped forward with their batons, ready to crash inside, when they heard Montoya. "That won't be necessary. Here's the key." He dangled it in the air with a peculiar smile on his face.

Thirteen

Bella Perez napped against the outside door to the Juarez Hospital and nearly toppled over when someone pushed it open from the inside.

A staff member in a long white coat glanced down on her lying on the concrete outside. "Come on in, doors open."

Bella couldn't believe the nerve of these people. Hospitals should stay open twenty four seven. She jumped to her feet, scrambled around to find a mirror to fix her hair. If anyone saw her in such condition, it would be the end of her rising career. With one hand on the door, she glanced in either direction and noticed Pedro still fast asleep further down on the sidewalk, leaning against a clump of bushes. She walked over, tugged on his sleeve. "Pedro. Wake up. They're letting us in."

"What? Huh?" He wiped his eyes and rolled over.

"Get your camera and let's get going. They're finally letting the media inside."

Pedro mumbled something under his breath, got his camera and followed her through the front doors.

"Good morning." She straightened her skirt and pulled it down. "I'm Bella Perez. Thank you for granting access—"

The woman at the circulation desk scowled. "What are you talking about?"

Bella turned to her cameraman. "Pedro, is film running?"

"*Si.*"

Bella turned back to the woman and smiled. "I'm here to interview the hospital spokesperson about *Presidente* Benito Juarez' condition."

The woman chuckled. "El Presidente left here late last night miss, I'm afraid you missed the scoop. Didn't you catch it on CNN?"

Bella twisted her face in an unladylike scowl and stomped to the door like a spoiled child. "Of all the nerve. Come on Pedro. We're leaving."

***

Benito sat at the small round table inside his private office with his father and Rita. He preferred this space to the larger room down the hall, primarily for added privacy. "Okay you two. What will I say today in the press conference?"

Juarez Senor growled. "You shouldn't do one at all."

Bene often grew weary from having to continually justify himself to his father. "Not an option. Rita, what are my people saying?"

Rita put on her reading glasses, pulled out a notebook and flipped through several pages of handwritten notes. "Well, we received several calls from around the city, the state, the country, and CNN called a few minutes ago. They're all asking the same questions."

"What?" Bene asked.

"Are you alive, was our government overthrown, and what went on last night in Cathedral Metropolitano."

"Understandable. I can handle them," Bene said.

"Two months in office and you're ready, huh?" his father asked.

Bene sighed. He would not dignify his father's sarcasm with a response. "What else, Rita?"

"They want to know who is responsible, an international terrorist or someone local and is the situation under control."

Juarez Senior sighed. "This is not a good idea."

"Father, I can't just sit here while our citizens believe our country is falling apart, now can I?"

Juarez grumbled. "Things are not under control. You of all people should know that."

"Maybe not, but we can't allow panic to ensue." Bene glanced out the window into the Zocalo. "Where's Mario right now?"

***

Salazar decided to continue pleading for his release. "Please don't hurt me. Let me go. God will forgive you, I promise."

"Shut up old man." The giant shoved Salazar across the dirt floor through a narrow passage.

Salazar had never seen this tunnel before in all his years of service to the church. They climbed up through a tight hole with built in stair steps on the mud walls probably used by the Aztecs themselves.

Out of breath, Salazar stopped for a brief moment. "Wait, I'm getting tired."

"Hurry up." The giant shoved him against the stone walls.

The elderly priest clutched his hand to his neck. "I…can't. I'm out of breath."

"You get going now if you want to live, Father."

Salazar tried to lift his leg, but it felt like lead. His head felt dizzy and pain tore through his chest. He heaved forward, vomiting white foam and nearly toppled over. Bracing himself against the stone wall, he slowly fell to his knees. "Agh, I think I'm having a heart attack."

Fourteen

Mario almost lost control and punched Dennis Montoya's lights out right then and there. Luckily he refrained. That wouldn't do anyone any good. If something sinister showed up today, he would get a warrant for Montoya's arrest immediately.

Montoya shuffled through the key ring and unlocked the heavy door. "Here you go."

"If you knew about this tunnel and had a key all along, why didn't you tell us before?"

Montoya smirked. "You never asked…"

"Get out of our way," Mario shouted. "You stay out of here, Montoya. I've had about enough of you."

Montoya raised his hands, stepped away from the door. "Fine. I'm going back to my office to make some phone calls. Help yourselves."

Mario pushed the heavy doors inward and revealed a great cavernous stone walled room with ceilings over twenty feet high. Several tapestries depicting Aztec gods hung on the walls, supported by thick wooden poles. "Boys, I think we found what we came for. Get busy and let's search every inch."

The other officers could hardly believe their eyes. "So what do you think this place is?"one of them asked.

"I don't know, but it can't be good." Mario walked around, shining his flashlight in every corner. On a far wall to the right, he found a slightly elevated stage area. Varied footprints outlined in the dirt floor, suggested dozens if not hundreds of people recently gathered here.

"What are we looking for?" an officer asked.

Mario fell to his knees on the stage, tracing the boards with his hands and searching for blood. "Doorways, hiding places where they could hide Salazar."

"Salazar?" Senora Sanchez asked. "What are you talking about?"

Mario couldn't believe Sanchez hadn't heard the news yet. "Si, last night someone tried to kill *El Presidente* and kidnapped Father Salazar in the process."

Senora Sanchez gasped, tears filled her eyes and she brought her hands to her mouth. "My God. I hope he's alright."

"I'm sure he will be, if we can find him soon. I'm hoping this search today will give us the evidence we need to bring him home safely."

Sanchez seemed shaken. "Father Salazar gave me my first Communion. I can't imagine who would want to hurt him."

Mario studied her, making sure she wasn't hiding something herself. "I will do my best to find him, Senora."

She sniffled and wiped her tears. "Well then, I won't bother you anymore. I'm sorry for doubting you. I should've let you come in here when you first asked."

"What's done is done."

"I hate this happened. If I'd let you in the other day, Father Salazar might still be around."

"You can't second guess yourself."

"Si, but I can't help but wonder…"

"Don't worry about it, *por favor*. Go on back to your office and try to relax."

"*Si, gracias.*"

"*Senor*," an officer called out. "I think we found something over here."

"Go back to your office, *senora*." Mario noticed Montoya was still busy on his cell phone. "And him too. Keep him out of here." He followed the officer to a far corner of the room where at least a hundred brown hooded robes hung neatly filling an entire wall.

The officer pulled one from the hook, twisted it around in his hands. "I don't know what to make of these, *senor*. Do you think they belong to monks from the cathedral?"

Mario picked one up and discovered a large dried blood spot on the left sleeve. "No officer, I don't. Take all of these down, bag them and enter them into evidence."

***

Bene picked up the phone and called Mario's cell. "Where are you, *amigo*?"

"Uh, I'm near Templo Mayor doing the search, why? What's up?"

"Three things," Bene said. "First, thank you for all you're doing, second, I'm planning an important press conference today at two and I need you here in my office by 1:45 at the very latest, and three—"

"*Si?*"

"I'm really hoping you have some good news to tell me about what you've found today."

"Actually, I'm glad you called. We just found a secret tunnel connecting the Templo Mayor to an underground Aztec ceremonial chamber of some kind."

"Really? Incredible." Bene gave his father and Rita the thumbs up sign.

"What did he say?" Juarez Senior interrupted.

Bene covered his palm on the receiver. "Dad, just a minute. I am trying to find out."

"What did your father say?" Mario asked.

"Oh nothing, my dad wants to know what you found."

"We're still trying to sort it all out. All I can say is there is something here and based on what I've seen so far, I believe this is where the killers took Rosa. They probably brought her through the restricted area in the Museo, through the tunnel and into this place. In fact, I would bet my life on it. Hopefully we can—"

"I found something." One of the officers shouted to Mario in the background. "It's a doorway." He kicked it in.

"Did I hear what I thought I heard?" Bene asked.

"Si. I need to go. I will call you when I know something for sure."

Bene hung up the phone.

"Well, what did he say?" Rita asked. "Did he find something?"

Benito didn't know what to make of it all, but he hoped it meant Salazar would come home soon. "*Si.*"

Juarez Senior leaned forward in his chair. "What?"

"He's not sure yet. Keep the press conference this afternoon, Rita. I have a good feeling we'll know something solid by then."

Fifteen

Amelia Sanchez almost broke a heel running back through the tunnel and into the Museo. She went straight for her office where Montoya sat behind her desk using the phone. She walked in and slammed the door. "We need to talk."

Montoya covered the receiver with his palm. "In a minute."

"No, now." Sanchez hung up his call.

He removed his glasses, and scowled. "Hey. What do you think you're doing?"

Sanchez lowered her voice. "Who do you think you are, Dennis? What kind of nonsense are you pulling around here?"

"I—"

"I don't know what kind of trouble you've gotten yourself into or who you're talking to, but I want no part of it. *Comprende?* You will stop coming in here, sitting at my desk and talking to your cronies."

Montoya pounded his fist on her desk, sending a stack of papers flying to the floor. "I am the Chairman of the Board."

Sanchez scooped her papers in her hands and dumped them in the center of the desk. "I don't care. Get your things and get out.   Don't come back until you've washed your hands of whatever mess you're into." She pointed to her door with a trembling hand.

"Fine." Montoya quickly slammed his things into a small briefcase. "You won't hear the end of this, Amelia. You'll be sorry for this." He pushed past her and slammed the door.

Amelia Sanchez leaned against her office door, turned the deadbolt and burst into tears. Something was wrong and she knew it. First Mario's sister, now *El Presidente* and her long time Priest Father Salazar. She pulled her Bible from her top drawer and prayed whoever did this had nothing to do with her organization.

***

Mario ran to the other side of the building where officers already kicked in the door of a cell containing a small cot, recently used chamber pot, and tiny table. On the floor, they found the most damning piece of evidence to date. "Look." Mario held it up so the officers could see.

"What is it?" The officers stepped closer.

"A collar worn only by a priest, and if I'm right, this one belongs to Father Salazar."

"How do you know that?" an officer asked.

Mario pointed out the fresh blood stains. His phone rang. His mother's number appeared on caller ID. "Bag this up, will you? Excuse me, I need to take this." He walked over to a corner. "Mama, I'm busy now. Can I call you back?"

Elsa sounded frenzied. "I'm planning Angela's funeral for tomorrow afternoon."

Mario's heart sank. He should be there, but he had an obligation to find Angela's killer. "I wish I could help, but right now—"

Elsa seemed in brighter spirits today, despite the upcoming funeral. "I handled everything. Sylvia's been a big help."

Mario hated this. "Call Benito's office and let him know, okay? You have the number, right?"

Silence.

"Mama?"

More silence.

Mario sighed. He understood his mother held a grudge against Benito, but the man loved his sister and in honor of her memory, needed to be treated like family. The longer these tensions remained, the harder it would be to heal, especially since Mario now considered Benito more brother than employer. Elsa was always stubborn, though, and he hoped she would put aside her differences and get along. "Mama, you call them and don't make me do it. Call right now. It would mean a lot to him, I know."

Elsa sighed. "Okay."

"Thank you, Mama. I love you."

"Love you," she said.

He returned to the men. "Listen gentlemen, if this is Salazar's collar, we're running out of time. Let's tear this place apart."

Sixteen

Sylvia Ortiz stepped out into the hall and quietly closed the door to her son's hospital room after a short conversation with him. Carlos was on the road to recovery and she was grateful for that. She walked down the hall, past the nurses' station, and into the waiting area, when someone passed her in the opposite direction.

***

The man in the unseasonably warm black leather jacket and sunglasses went completely unnoticed by Ortiz and the nurses who were busy reading charts and tending patients to pay attention to much else.

He cracked open the door, saw the young boy resting peacefully, his monitors steadily keeping the rhythm of his ever strengthening heartbeat.

The man stepped closer, careful not to wake him, and removed the hypodermic needle from the inside breast pocket of his jacket. He reached for Carlos' IV and carefully, with the precision of a well-trained surgeon, shot the fluid into his veins.

At that moment, Carlos Ortiz opened his eyes and gasped.

***

Bella Perez and Pedro returned to the Zocalo just in time to see dozens of television trucks already parked all along the street near the Palacio. She slammed her hands on the dash. "Hurry and park. We've got to get set up."

Pedro pulled into the center of the Zocalo. Several remote satellites blocked the way, along with the bleachers assembled for some kind of gathering.

Bella pushed her way through the throngs of reporters and news crews until she hit the front line. "Excuse me, excuse me…"

A tall man stepped toward her and pushed her back. "No further access ma'am."

"What do you mean? Don't you know who I am?"

The man wrinkled his nose. "No."

Bella puffed her shoulders back, straightened her jacket a bit. "*Bella Perez*?"

He shrugged. "We're told only CNN has access to this area."

Bella was sick and tired of hearing about CNN. What did they know? They weren't the heartbeat of Mexico City – she was, and she demanded respect. "CNN? What are you talking about? I cover local events. What's going on?"

"*El Presidente* scheduled a press conference for this afternoon," the man told her.

She put on her best pout ."Yeah, but I was here first."

The man laughed. "I don't think so, miss. Now step back or I'll have to force you to do so."

Bella stomped her heels and her aching feet on the cobblestones, nearly twisting her ankle as she turned to go find Pedro. Right now she needed a good shoulder to cry on.

***

Bene Juarez stared down into the Zocalo where thousands of people gathered to hear the upcoming press conference. Dozens of media trucks with satellites mounted on top made the place appear more like a sporting event than a political one. "I can't believe all the people down there."

Juarez Senior pat his son on the back. "*Si,* they want to make sure you're alive. You were right."

Bene's stomach tightened. He hoped he wouldn't freeze up or forget what to say. "I've never spoken to such a large crowd before."

"You'll do fine," Juarez Senior said.

"*Senor?*" Rita knocked. "They're ready for you. Should I send them in?"

"*Si.*"

A young woman entered carrying a supply kit filled with makeup and hair product. Bene took a seat in his chair while she busily plastered foundation and powder on his face. He felt uneasy after recent events and the people who drugged him and forced him to disguise himself. He wanted to press those memories from his mind, although he also felt ashamed. Any pain he endured paled in comparison to what those monsters did to his Angel in her final moments on Earth. His eyes filled with tears. He couldn't think about Angela now. "Is this necessary?"

The woman dabbed his nose with a sponge. "*Si.* All the *Presidente's* wear makeup so they look better on TV. Otherwise you'll be shiny. We can't have our Presidente looking shiny, now can we?"

Bene chuckled not knowing whether to take that as a compliment or an insult.

"One thing's for sure, Bene," his father said. "It helps with that cut on your head."

With everything happening, Benito nearly forgot the gash on his head. The makeup artist was right. The public needed to believe he was okay, and that cut would not inspire confidence. He closed his eyes, and kept quiet until she finished. Then he reached for a hand held mirror to take a look. He tipped his head to the side and noticed the gash magically disappeared. "I guess you're right on that one, Father. I do look better now. That's good, because I don't want anyone to know how bad this situation is."

Juarez senior agreed. "*Si*, with any kind of luck, the whole mess will be cleared up before anyone has to find out otherwise."

Bene wondered about Mario. He hadn't heard from him in hours. He prayed the discoveries he made earlier meant Father Salazar would come home soon. "Speaking of that, I want Mario by my side today. I want the people to know who took care of this situation for them and that everything is okay now."

"But it's not yet," his father said.

"Have faith, Father. It will be."

Juarez Senior sighed. "I'm not sure if that's such a good idea, son. What if—"

"In this matter I will not change my mind. The people need a face to relate to as the hero who saved their Presidente. Mario will stand with me today. He is the hero we all need right now. End of discussion."

***

Carlos opened his eyes and stared at the tall man in a black leather jacket who wanted him dead. The sting from the injection burned through his veins and jogged him awake.

Eyes wide open, he wanted to scream, but couldn't speak above a whisper thanks to the hole in his stomach. He cried out slightly, but realized nobody outside his room could hear him.

The last image Carlos saw was the Mylar balloon bouquet his mother brought him moments earlier. He always liked balloons.

Like a helium balloon soaring far away from its owner, Carlos Ortiz drifted into the hereafter to the sound of a loud and steady tone.

***

The man waited until cardiac arrest registered on the monitor. Once the boy's death was confirmed, the alarm sounded, and the man quietly slipped out of the hospital room. He walked slowly past five nurses running down the hall to check on Carlos Ortiz.

He stepped on the elevator and left the building through the front door. He smiled. Job well done.

Seventeen

The police officers dismantled the cot in the underground cell, swabbing it for any DNA or blood. They took dirt samples from the floors, photographed the entire area and bagged evidence including the priest collar.

Mario studied the cell and thought of poor Father Salazar. Their first meeting wasn't exactly under the best of circumstances, but he felt sorry him just the same.

Montoya stood out in the main hall talking to one of his officers dangling the bag containing the priest collar in his fingers. "There is no way this belongs to Father Salazar. Impossible."

Mario clenched his teeth and stormed toward them. "I thought I told you to stay out of here. And what are you doing handling my evidence? Give that back to the officer now."

Montoya stood his ground even though he was half Mario's size. "I need to supervise you and make sure you aren't destroying property."

Mario couldn't believe Montoya's arrogance. He grabbed the collar from his hands, held it up and pointed out the blood stain. "Did you see this?"

"So? That still doesn't link it to Salazar. Any number of people could have left it behind."

Mario handed the collar back to his investigator, walked over and shoved Montoya into the wall. "You better hope it doesn't, *senor,* or next time I show up, I'll have a warrant with your name on it."

Senora Sanchez' eyes blazed hot. "Dennis, what are you doing here? I thought I sent you home."

Montoya chuckled. "You can't tell me what to do, *senora.* I'm your boss, remember?"

Senora Sanchez ran up to Montoya and grabbed the sleeve of his suit jacket. "Stop. Let them do their job."

"But—" Montoya jerked his arm away.

"But nothing," Sanchez huffed then turned to Mario. "I don't know what's going on around here. I swear I never knew a thing about the tunnel before today."

Mario raised his eyebrow at her. Surely she knew something. His hope of Sanchez' innocence instantly diminished. "Really?"

"I swear it."' Her face registered real emotion, her eyes watered. "I've known Father Salazar my whole life. I'd do anything to help him."

"I'll do what I can to bring him back safely, but it would be a great help if you could get him…" Mario pointed to Montoya. "…out of here. Now, *por favor*. And make sure he stays out this time."

Sanchez grabbed Montoya's arm and led him out. "Come on Dennis. Let's go back before a *Museo* guest finds the tunnel. I left the door open."

"It's my right to be here," Montoya protested.

"No it isn't," Sanchez said. "Remember? We have an agreement. You mind your own business from now on."

Montoya's face reddened. "You listen to me. I am chairman of the Board."

"And I am curator, and if you don't like it, I am happy to tender my resignation effective immediately."

"No—"

"Then come on *Senor* Montoya. Give these men some space." Sanchez pulled Montoya's sleeve and led him back through the tunnel.

One officer turned to Mario, shook his head. "Man are they a mess."

Mario watched them leave. "I don't trust that man as far as I can throw him. Keep searching. We need to find anything and everything we can if we expect to find the Father alive."

Eighteen

Mario kept searching the underground cavern for clues and discovered two more small rooms with nothing consequential in either one of them. He walked back out to the main assembly hall, glanced at the stage. Three stone steps led up to the main platform, and above it, two small stone altars flanked each side of the main podium and typical steps reminiscent of the ancient Aztecs led up to the top. He tried to imagine hundreds of people gathered all around, like last night in the Cathedral Metropolitano, only down here, they were out of public view.

He remembered the crazy Circuit Court Judge Pena. He would likely stand on the stage to perform any ritual acts, probably right next to the largest stone platform. Mario crossed the room slowly, trying to get the feeling of being in the crowd, what they might see, hear and do, always careful to check the ground for signs of blood. At first, he found none.

Directly in front of the platform, he saw bright red dried paint dripping over on to the dirt. *Paint or something else?* His officers would need to collect dirt samples for the lab. He took a few steps backward, keeping his eyes on the tunnel door, when he tripped over something and fell.

Thinking it was a rubber ball, or piece of trash, he picked it up, and screamed. "Agh."

Ten huge men ran toward him. "What's up, Mario?"

He dropped the thing on the platform out of mere shock. Once he took a closer look, his eyes watered, his heart filled with rage. "Why? Can you tell me why? Look at this." He carefully picked up the tiny body of a fetus not more than a few months old. "What kind of monsters are we dealing with? Please tell me."

The officers were visibly shaken.

Mario scooped the tiny infant into his hands, unable to understand such violence. He picked up a clean piece of white cloth, carefully wrapping the child in it out of respect, the kind of respect any mother would want shown to her baby. The idea that pregnant women were being slaughtered down here made his head spin. No matter what it took, he would find these people and kill every one of them himself if necessary. "I want this taken to the lab and tested today, do you hear me?"

"Si," the officers nodded.

"Get me dirt samples from this area here." He pointed to the spots he found. "Scrape this stone here, and there..."

"Right away, *senor,*" another officer said.

"We need to get this tested and get results back immediately." Mario glanced at his watch. Benito's press conference started soon and he promised to be there, even though he needed to oversee the investigation too. "I have to go. You guys take care of this and I'll be back when I can."

***

Bene knew something was wrong with Mario the minute he stepped into his office.

His eyes were bloodshot and watery. He panted from exhaustion. "Sorry I'm late."

"You're not late." Bene pointed to the clock.

"I am five minutes late, Bene."

Bene smiled. "No problemo. We have a few minutes until I need to be outside. Sit down."

"Thanks." Mario took a seat and stared at Bene for a second. "Hey, you shaved. Looks good."

Bene rubbed his smooth chin. "Like it? I thought it might help after what you told me about *Quetzalcoatl*."

"I hope so." Mario sat at the round table, his smile quickly faded.

"What is it? What's wrong?"

Mario sighed. "I don't know if you want to hear this or not. You have a lot on your mind right now and…"

"What is it?"

"You wanted me to bring you news of a breakthrough in this case, but I don't have one yet."

"That's fine. I don't expect a miracle, you know."

"You should," Mario said. "Father Salazar needs one right about now."

"Is there something else I should know about?"

Mario sighed. "I can tell you in a little while after you speak today. Not now. We found something today, but you need to stay positive. The people need to know they are safe."

"Are they?" Bene asked.

Mario stared him directly in the eye and slowly shook his head.

***

Bella pressed her body against the crowd, trying her best to scoot closer to where Presidente Juarez would give his speech. If it wouldn't cause her make up to smear, she would start crying right here and now, but she couldn't just yet. She needed to keep herself together and get this story. "Get me that crate from the back," she ordered the grip.

He returned a moment later and handed it to her. "Here you go." He smiled like a love-struck schoolboy.

"Give me that." She put it on the ground and stepped up on it, hoping to add some height, but her heel got caught, she slipped and fell over, nearly hitting some spectators and tearing a hole in her new dress. "Agh. Will this nightmare ever end?"

Pedro chuckled quietly behind the lens of the camera.

"Hey. You better not be filming this, you hear me?"

Nineteen

Bene stood outside in the hot afternoon sun with the Palacio in the background. He glanced out over the thousands gathered in the Zocalo and began his speech. All the nerves he felt earlier faded away. He felt a level of confidence similar to what he experienced when running for office. *Look into the camera, be sincere.* "Ladies and gentlemen, thank you for coming out today. I called this press conference to explain the incidents of last evening, and to assure the Mexican people and our allied countries I am alive and well, and Mexico is strong."

Behind the bleachers, reserved for media only, crowds of people started gathering to listen to the historic Presidential speech.

"In fact, since taking office less than two months ago, this is my first formal press conference, and I am excited about the direction our country is going, and proud to call myself a citizen of Mexico."

The gathered crowd cheered and waved for the cameras.

"Last night, an incident unfolded in Cathedral Metropolitano involving some citizens. We recovered the bodies of two murder victims. While this is tragic and the investigation is ongoing, I'm relieved to say there were no serious injuries during the incident."

The crowd applauded.

Bene cleared his throat, prepared for the more serious part of the speech. "I want to clarify rumors. I was at the Cathedral last night but I'm fine and this incident is isolated and contained."

The crowd applauded, but then grew still.

He continued. "Once again let me clarify, authorities apprehended the people responsible for last night's unfortunate event and they are no longer a threat to Mexico City."

Everyone broke out in thunderous applause.

"*Mis amigos*, I am proud to say Mario Martinez here," Bene turned slightly to his right and slapped Mario on the back. "…personally apprehended these suspects, and is now leading our internal investigation. Everything is under complete control, and now I will take your questions."

A few hundred hands went up at once.

"Yes?" Bene pointed to a reporter from CNN.

"*Senor Presidente*, how many gunmen were inside the Cathedral last night? Are they in jail? Did you capture them all?"

"*Si.* All of the gunmen were shot and none survived." He pointed to another reporter. "*Si?*"

"*Presidente* Juarez, are you certain the threat is over since you obviously have no suspects in custody?"

Bene nodded and smiled. "Si. Our initial investigation suggests a local group is responsible."

"Don't you mean a gang?" a reporter asked.

Bene didn't realize how tough the media would be. He tried not to openly sigh and give off any appearance of frustration. "I don't believe so, but I'm not at liberty to say. We're looking into it. Okay, I have time for one more question." He pointed to a man in the back row who wore a black leather jacket. "You."

"*Senor Presidente*, if this crime wasn't gang related, are you telling the people of our city this crime was committed by a completely random group of men?"

"*Si.*"

"And you believe you apprehended them all, do you?"

"*Si.*"

"What if you didn't?"

Bene got a cold chill up his spine. "I am told from good sources the situation is handled. Now if you will excuse me, I thank you all for being here today." He smiled and waved at the hundreds of flashing cameras, and stepped into the safety of his entourage and out of sight.

***

Mario watched the man in the black leather jacket with great interest while he disappeared into the crowd. He knew one thing for sure, that man was no reporter.

"Mario. Mario." Bella clicked across the concrete wearing the same skin tight lime green dress with the front cut down to her naval she had on last night. Her hair was a knotted mess, and she had a smudge of dirt across her right cheek. She waved her arms frantically and ran toward him.

He waved back at her. "Later, okay?" Before he could take any questions from Bella or anyone else, Mario felt himself pressed up against the bodies of the secret service guards who ushered him and Bene back inside the Palacio, up the stairs.

Back in Bene's office, his father welcomed them inside and closed the door behind them and poured everyone a scotch on the rocks. "Good job, son. You made me proud."

"Thank you, father," Bene took the glass raised his. "To Mario."

Juarez lifted his glass. "To Mario, and I actually like the shave too, now that I think about it."

Benito chuckled and took another sip. "Told you it would grow on you." Bene glanced at Mario. "What's wrong? You look like someone just died."

Mario couldn't drink or cheer right now. Not with cold hearted killers on the loose who targeted babies and priests. He stared down at the floor wondering if he should tell Bene now about the fetus and wreck the good mood or not. There were so few things to celebrate lately, he hated to be the bearer of any more bad news. "Nothing."

"Don't say nothing. You've been upset about something since you got here today, so tell me, amigo. What is it?"

Mario sighed. "You are a true politician, aren't you, Benito?"

Bene scowled. "What do you mean?"

Mario shuffled his feet on the carpet. "Nothing."

"What? Tell me."

"You know good and well everything you said out there was a lie. You're completely full of it. I thought you were different, but I can see you're not. You tell the people what they want to hear, that's it."

"Yes, but—"

"But what? You want those people to think that I saved the day last night? Huh?"

"But essentially you did, Mario, and besides, I can't allow people to panic, can I?"

"You lied to the people of Mexico, Bene. Don't you see that? Those men in the Cathedral last night weren't armed with guns. *They carried spears.* Obsidian tipped spears like the ones the Aztecs used back in the 1500's." His face felt hot and he knew he needed to hold his tongue. He shook his head, tried to calm down. "I'm sorry, but you have no idea what we're dealing with here. If you did…"

"Is that it?" Juarez Senior asked.

"Dad, please, let Mario talk." Bene turned to Mario. "Go ahead."

"No, *Senor* Juarez is right. I'd better stop while I'm ahead."

"Good man," Juarez Senior said.

"Dad." Bene held his hand up at his father. "Go on. I am serious when I say you are my brother and you can tell me anything, even if I don't like it and don't want to hear it."

Mario took a breath to keep from shouting, "You have no idea what we found today inside that underground chamber. If you did, you would realize we are nowhere near finding the bastards who did this to you, and to who knows who else." Mario held his forehead in his hands. "I can't believe you told our people I could save them. My God, Bene! How could you?"

"But you can, Mario." Bene said. "You saved me, didn't you?"

"I got lucky. That's it."

"I have faith in you. I know you will bring Father Salazar back in one piece. I just know it."

"Well that makes one of us."

"Why don't you tell us what you saw today?" Juarez Senor asked.

Mario's cell rang. "Just a moment." He turned to answer, "Hola?" As he listened to the man on the other end of the line, his blood ran cold. He hung up.

"Who was that?" Bene asked.

Mario felt ill. "I have to go. I will tell you everything in a bit, but right now they need me over at the cathedral. They found something else."

Twenty

Sylvia Ortiz was right outside Carlos' door reading a magazine when she happened to overhear the trauma unit rushing to his room. She raced down the hall, practically knocking over a nurses cart in the process and when she arrived in his room, her son already turned blue.

"Get out of the way," one of the emergency workers shouted.

They shoved her aside and she watched helplessly while the team of doctors and nurses unsuccessfully attempt to revive her son. "Please. Do something. You have to save my baby."

After five unsuccessful attempts with the crash cart, the attending doctor called the time of death.

Sylvia leaned her back against the wall until her knees began to give out and she slowly sunk to the floor, collapsing into tears.

***

Father Salazar fell backwards down the tunnel, let go of his hold on the ladder, and landed on top of his startled captor. "Please. Help me. I think I'm having a heart attack."

The giant tried to push him forward in the tunnel when he fell and wound up catching him. He rushed down the steps, carrying the priest in his arms. "Are you serious? Are you sure you aren't lying?"

One good look at the priest said otherwise. The giant turned his head when he heard the shouts and voices from the room next door. They were nearly out of time. If they didn't leave right now, chances were pretty good someone would find them in here. He flung Salazar over his shoulder and lifted him up the stairs, much as one would lift a sack of rice.

In the background, he heard men working. Too close for comfort. They needed to get out of here. Nobody should be in here today, so if they were within hearing range, something was wrong. He hurried down the tunnel while the priest dribbled all over his shirt.

Out of breath, but not out of strength, the giant finally reached the top of the stairs. He cinched Salazar's limp body higher on his shoulders, and ran down the long corridor through the back section of Cathedral Metropolitano. He hoped the nuns wouldn't see them either, but fortunately nobody showed their face. Finally the giant reached the back door and ran down the alley where he parked his car earlier that afternoon. He kept the doors unlocked, luckily, in case he needed a quick escape, and flung the ailing priest on the back seat, "Don't worry, Father. I will get you some help."

Father Salazar didn't look good. His skin turned a strange shade of green and his skin felt cold, wet and sweaty, all at once. His breathing was labored and when the car started, Salazar turned on his side and threw up again.

The giant glanced back in his rearview mirror and caught the priest throwing up, ruining his new floor mats. This was not good.

Within five minutes, the giant pulled up in front of the closest hospital, pulled around to the emergency room entrance and left his car running as he carried the priest through the doors and yelled. "Heart attack. Quick. Someone help."

Once he saw several orderlies rushing toward them, the giant dropped Salazar on the linoleum floor and ran back to his car, screeching away before anyone could stop him. The powers that be wouldn't be pleased about this situation, or his chosen outcome, the giant realized, but at the moment, he didn't really care. He wasn't going to let the priest die, not like this anyway.

Just around the block from the hospital, he picked up his cell and called the only person he thought could help him.

***

The executive shut off his office lights, about to leave for the day, when his private cell rang. He immediately recognized the caller ID. "Hola?"

"Papa. I need to tell you—"

"Did you take care of it? You made it out of town okay, *si*?"

"That's why I'm calling. The priest, Papa, he started having a heart attack right when I tried to move him. I panicked. I didn't know what to do."

The Executive was disappointed. They would need a replacement. "It's okay, son. He would have died anyway. There is nothing you could do. We won't bring him to our next meeting...or maybe we could—"

"No, Papa. You don't understand. He's not with me anymore."

The executive thought he misunderstood his normally capable first born. "What do you mean?"

"I couldn't let him suffer. He threw up all over my new floor mats, he turned weird colors. I didn't know what to do."

"So what did you do with him?"

"I...I took him to the emergency room."

"Que? What are you talking about? Are you out of your mind?"

"No. It's not like that. I pulled up and dumped him in the emergency room lobby. Nobody saw me, I swear."

The Executive felt the vein in the side of his neck bulge under his shirt collar and tie. "How could you be so stupido? Do you not realize those places have cameras?"

"I'm sorry. I didn't know what to do." His son started to cry. "I couldn't just sit there and let him suffer such a terrible death, could I? He's our priest. He gave me my first Communion."

The executive took a letter opener from the top drawer of his desk and sliced a page from his appointment book. "Son, I swear if we weren't related, I would kill you right now. Literally." *And I probably will anyway...*

"Sorry, really I am."

"Stop whining. What's done is done. Once you're finished with your sniveling, you get back to the house, okay?"

"*Si*, I'm on my way."

"Where are you right now?"

"In the Zocalo on the far end near the Cathedral."

"Perfect. Stay right where you are and I'll come get you. What are you wearing today?"

"Jeans, black t-shirt."

"On second thought, why don't you wait on the Cathedral steps for me so I can find you easier. Think you can do that?"

"*Si.*"

"Wonderful. Go now. I'll be right there." The Executive turned his office light back on, sat at his desk and made another quick call.

Twenty One

Mario rushed back to the tunnel under Templo Mayor. By the time he arrived, the officers installed sophisticated forensics equipment to help analyze evidence.

"Martinez, come over here and I'll show you."

He hoped they hadn't found anything new while he'd been at the press conference this afternoon, especially nothing like what he heard about on the phone a few minutes ago. He didn't know if he could handle seeing anymore handy work of the maniacs who kidnapped Bene and Father Salazar. He followed the officer into the far corner near the platform where he found the fetus earlier that afternoon. There, folded and crumpled underneath the stage area lay the body of a young child decomposed so badly, they couldn't tell if it was a boy or girl without running tests. Mario clasped his hand over his mouth and turned away, shaking his head, trying not to let the image sink too far into his mind.

"I told them not to move it until you could see," the officer said.

"You did the right thing," Mario told him. "I just…don't know what to do about any of this. It's far worse than I ever imagined."

"*Si*. What will we tell the mother, I wonder?" the officer asked. "That is if we could even find her. If he never went to a dentist, we won't ever identify him."

They would need to put a bulletin on the news, but before releasing any sensitive information about the case, he would need to check with Bene first. "What I want to know is what we will tell the family of the poor woman who they sliced open to get that fetus. Now that would be a terrible phone call to make."

"*Si*, you're not kidding." the officer nodded.

For the next few hours, Mario watched the team bag the remains of the child, finish collecting blood samples, and scouring the area again to check for anything they missed. He yawned. After several days of no sleep, exhaustion finally started to take a toll. His phone rang. "Hola?"

"It's Bene. Rita spoke with your mother today about Angela's funeral tomorrow and I wanted you to know I will be there, and…"

Mario yawned again. He forgot all about his sister's funeral which was the main reason he worked so hard in the first place. "*Si*, okay, but we still haven't found Salazar yet, and I'm worried." He yawned again, only louder. "We ran into some other things here we're looking at first."

"Hey. I heard that." Bene said.

"Heard what?"

"You know what."

Mario gulped. "Am I in trouble?"

Bene chuckled. "No. Not yet, anyway. Why don't you go home, get some sleep, and go at it again in the morning?"

"How can I? Salazar is still out there somewhere. I can't rest until I find him, plus we've found some disturbing things here I need to tell you about." He yawned again.

"You found me, right? I know you will find Salazar too, but not if you can't stay awake."

"You are one to talk. I thought you needed to get rest."

Bene chuckled. "Are you kidding? Those maniacs kept me so doped up, I did nothing but sleep for three days straight. Go home, *por favor*."

Mario walked into the far corner of the cavern, away from everyone else. "You need to get another team to go out to the *Santa Cecilia Acatitlan* site today. The cult was out there the day before I found you doing who knows what."

"I can't do that today."

"Why not? Based on what we've found here today and what Carlos said, I have a hunch Ricardo's body may be out there too, along with remains of possibly several other people and who knows what other evidence. I went out there and saw far more blood evidence than anything we've seen here today, and…"

"The forensics people I assigned to you will be working around the clock on this, so while we wait to see, you need to rest up. Then I want you back at it, and hopefully by tomorrow, we will know where Salazar is being kept."

"We need to take care of it now, Bene, today. The forensics team is here with me now, and they're almost finished, but we need to look in both locations."

"Tomorrow, *amigo*."

"I don't get it. We need to hurry."

"It's already past five now."

Mario glanced at his watch. "You've got to be kidding."

"Time flies, you know."

"I don't mind working all night."

"No my friend. The policia here in the city tend to get cranky if they work more than an eight hours shift, and besides, it will all be there tomorrow when everyone is fresh and there's enough light to see."

"We've still got two hours or more worth of light left today."

"Mario," Bene chuckled. "I know you want to find Angela's killers, I do to, but you are tired. Please get some rest. Do it for me and for Angela."

Mario sighed. Bene was right, but he hated to stop now. "Okay. I will go home. Tomorrow can I meet you and your father again in your office first thing, okay? I need to go over some of this evidence with you. I hope to have concrete answers by then."

"Hasta manana." Before Mario could protest any further, Bene hung up.

***

Outside in the center of the Zocalo, Ramon the Healer saw Mario Martinez across La Plaza de la Constitution. He turned to his long line of potential customers."I'll be right back," He took off running. "Mario." Martinez didn't hear him at first, so he tried again. "Mario Martinez."

Mario turned and jogged to a stop. "Ramon. *Que pasa?*"

Ramon caught up to him and slugged him in the arm. "What do you mean, *Que pasa, man?* You never brought my car back. What's up?"

Mario slapped his forehead. "Oh yeah, about that…"

"I slept outside last night on a bench, *amigo*. Do you know how dangerous that is?"

"Look, Ramón, I know where your car is at," Mario began. "Or I should say where I left it last night—"

"What? You *left it last night*? What about the parking garage?"

Mario sighed. "*Si*, uh, let's just say a lot happened last night."

"I don't care, I need my car now."

"I can't get it for you right now, but tomorrow…"

"Oh yes you will, *amigo*. You will get it for me pronto. I am going to get my can of cash and we will go right now." Before Mario could respond, Ramón took off running.

Twenty Two

Mario waited impatiently while Ramon ran across the Zocalo to get his stuff. He hated having to ditch the healer's car last night, but he thought he could find it easily enough. He wrote down the name of the Metro Station where he left it. He needed to get home and get to bed and wished he could do this later.

Ramon ran up carrying a sack of what looked like cash from the day. "Okay boss. I'm ready to go when you are."

The sound of gunshots and screams filled the Zocalo. Mario spun around and saw a black car with tinted windows speeding away around a corner, and dozens of people rushing toward the Cathedral.

"Uh oh," Ramon said.

"You know what this means, Ramon. I'll catch you later," Mario called one of the Presidential approved officers who worked with him this morning and then ran toward the victim.

"Wait. I'm coming with you." Ramon ran after him.

At the base of the Cathedral Metropolitano steps lay the body of a young man probably around his same age, maybe a year or two younger, shot several times in the chest and stomach from close range from a semi-automatic weapon. Mario leaned down and checked his pulse, but it was too late. He checked his pockets to see if he had any identification. They were empty except for a few pesos.

The victim's entire body was covered in tattoos. Thick black rings circled his neck, and his arms were covered in pictures of blue feathers. The words of Carlos echoed in his mind: *a giant covered in tattoos.* He took out his cell and quickly snapped a photo of the victim and slipped it back into his pocket just as several *policia* approached. Tomorrow he could show this to Carlos, see if this was the same man who paid him the money.

Mario got out of their way while the ambulance and paramedics arrived on the scene also. They tried to revive the young man repeatedly before finally bagging him and carrying him away.

"Wait a minute," Mario told his officer while several others approached. He picked up a used gum wrapper, scribbling on it. "Take my number and call when you've ID'd him. I think this has something to do with the case from last night, but I'm not sure. It's a hunch."

"Okay, will do," the officer tucked the paper in his shirt pocket.

Mario turned around and watched the stunned public whispering and pointing at the spot where the body lay moments earlier.

Someone pushing their way through the growing mob and once she came closer, he'd recognize those high heels anywhere. "What are you doing here? You're such an ambulance chaser you stay up all night long without even bothering to change?"

Bella scowled and pushed her long fingernail into his chest. "Are you ready to give me the information you promised me, Mario? You obviously know a lot since you're best friends with *El Presidente*."

"That's not true."

She clicked her long nails together. "That's the latest word on the streets these days."

"Well it isn't true and if that's the kind of news you report, I'm not saying a word."

"If you aren't talking, then get out of my way." Bella straightened her hair and walked right past him so she could stand right next to the fresh blood on the stone steps. "Good evening, I'm Bella Perez with breaking news. Tonight, only moments ago, the body of a young man was found brutally shot to death in the same place where violence erupted last night. In his speech today, Presidente Juarez claimed the violence was over. Did he lie?"

Mario shook his head. What a drama queen. He did agree with her though, Benito lied. He would never betray those inner thoughts to her though. He turned around, walked off.

"Hey." Ramon came running up after him. "What about my car?"

"Alright, Ramón. Let's go get the car."

"Can we stop by McDonald's first?"

Ramon was a bit of a pain in the ass, but Mario was hungry too. Might as well help someone less fortunate. "I guess. I suppose you want an apple pie too?"

"Of course."

Mario rolled his eyes. "Alright, come on."
***

The emergency room staff at the local hospital discovered Salazar immediately, but because of his recent ordeal, fresh bruises and missing priest's collar, nobody recognized him.

After he arrived at the hospital, the staff rushed the latest John Doe to emergency open heart surgery where he spent the next several hours having two blocked arteries repaired. The staff wheeled him into the intensive care unit recovery room where the placard on his door said nothing but *John Doe #3.*

"Who do you think he is?" one nurse asked another.

"I don't know, but whoever he is, he's lucky some Good Samaritan thought to drop him off when he did, or the old man would've been in heaven tonight."

"*Si*, you're not kidding," the other agreed.

They closed his door and went to finish their rounds.
***

"I suppose you saw the news tonight?"

The executive lowered the volume on his television set at home and whispered into the receiver of his cell phone. "Si."

"Then you know I took care of what you asked."

"Si, gracias. I never thought I would do that, but he gave me no choice."

"It's only a matter of time before they ID him, you know."

"We will cross that bridge when we get there. It may look like drugs."

"*Si*, but what about the priest?"

"I'm not sure yet."

"We could just slip into his hospital room and—"

"No we can't. We already visited a hospital today, remember? No, I want to plan something special to send a message they will not soon forget. Once our new leader is in place we will devise something far more elaborate for the Father Salazar and his Spaniard friends."

"What do you have in mind?"

"Now, now. Patience, *mi amigo*. Not too much longer. Goodbye." He hung up the phone.

The footage from the Presidential press conference popped up on the screen and there, front and center stood the man who singlehandedly screwed up everyone's plans - *Mario Martinez.* Soon that trouble maker would need to be dealt with too. He changed the channel when his wife came out of the kitchen with two iced cold Coronas and a steaming bowl of popcorn.

She sat next to him on the couch. "Who was that?"

He scooped the popcorn into his mouth, put his free arm around his wife. "Wrong number."

Twenty Three

By the time Mario and Ramon ate and climbed aboard the Metro, his cell rang.

"Mario. What's going on out there today?" Bene sounded panicked, upset. "I saw you on the news just now."

He cupped the phone with his hand to hear. "Another young man was gunned down in front of the Cathedral right when I left to go home."

"You don't think it was related to our other problem, do you?"

"The kid had a tattoo similar to Ricardo, so even though I want to believe it was drug or gang related, it's not., to me. I have one of the men checking on it. He said he'll call me once they make a positive ID on the victim."

"Si, it must be related," Bene said. "Okay, sorry to bother you. See you in the morning."

Mario hung up, his phone rang again. He picked it up without looking. "Si, Bene."

"Mario. This is your mother."

He felt a sinking feeling in his stomach. She didn't sound good. "What's wrong?"

"Carlos," she cried.

"What about him?"

"He's…dead," she sobbed.

"No!"

"Si," Elsa sniffed.

"What? I thought he was getting better."

She blubbered something he could not understand, then said, "Someone murdered him today in the hospital."

"Are you sure it was murder? His injuries were pretty severe, Mama."

"Si. He went into cardiac arrest this afternoon. The doctors said someone tampered with his IV."

Mario pressed his fingers on his temples. "Oh no. How is Sylvia?"

"She's here with me at the house. She's not doing so good."

"*Your* house?"

"Si."

A cold chill ran through his body. "Mama, I am still downtown, but I'm on my way. I want you and Sylvia to stay inside the house until I get there. And do not, I repeat *do not* answer the door for anyone, under any circumstances, *comprende*?"

"*Si*, but what's wrong?"

Mario didn't want to panic her by telling her about the other murders. "I will call you once I get off the Metro to tell you I'm nearby, but do not answer the door, no matter what. Promise me."

"Mario, you're scaring me."

"I'm sorry, Mama, I don't mean to scare you, but it's obvious someone knows where we live. You stay put until I can get there and get you two out."

"But…"

"Do it, Mama. Stay inside. Lock up. I'm on my way." Mario hung up and turned to Ramon. "Sorry, but McDonald's is out of the question."

***

Benito hung up the phone and turned to his father. "Mario says he isn't sure if the shooting today is related to my kidnapping, but it sounds like it might be."

Juarez Senior turned off the television. "Benito, there is nothing you can do about it tonight, so relax."

"Si, I know I can't do anything about it, but how can I relax when people are getting gunned down in the streets? What is this world coming to?"

Juarez Senior poured them both a scotch. "Here. This will help."

They clicked their glasses and drank.

"I know one thing for sure."

"What's that?" Bene asked between sips.

"It's good to have you back. I hardly knew what to do without my evening drink companion."

"I had enough mind altering substances to last a lifetime these past few days, but I must say, this scotch tastes better than ever tonight. Cheers."

"Cheers."

"To peace and the return of our dear friend, Father Salazar," Bene said.

"I'll drink to that," Juarez Senior tipped it back, draining the glass and slammed it on the bar.

"Wow, dad, you sure are drinking fast this evening."

"I've needed a good stiff drink lately."

"Si, I can't help but think the shooting is somehow related. I just wish..."

"What?"

"I wish I could bring peace to this city it so deserves. I would do anything to end crime and to see our people united as one."

"If anyone can do it, Bene, you can."

"If there's anyone we should drink to tonight, it's not me, it's Mario Martinez. If I succeed in making Mexico peaceful and safe, he will be a big part of it."

Juarez poured himself another glass, lifted it. "To Mario Martinez."

"Now I'll drink to that gladly." Bene smiled.

***

Of all the things that went wrong that day, something finally went Mario's way when he spotted Ramon's car parked in the exact same spot where he left it a little over twenty four hours ago. "Here you go." He reached in his pocket and handed him the keys.

"*Gracias, amigo.*"

"Listen, Ramon, I might need you to help me with a few more things, if you think you can spare some time."

Ramon nodded. "Si, of course. You know where my office is."

"I'm not sure what yet, but I have a feeling you might be able to help me later on."

Ramon shrugged. "Okay, you come and find me."

He shook the healer's hand, patted him on the shoulder. "Thank you bro. I'll be in touch."

Mario walked across the street and went back into the Metro station. He saw the newspaper on the stand and right there on the front cover Benito Juarez stood waving his hands at the crowd with him in the background. The headline read: *Presidente Optimistic Crime Spree Contained*

Mario cringed and ran down the stairs into the tunnel to catch the first train to his mother's house. He hated taking the Metro at rush hour, especially this particular line because his mother lived so far out from the city center, he sat in the cramped cars for nearly the entire ride before it finally began to clear out. Today he got lucky and found a seat next to an elderly woman carrying a shopping bag. His phone rang. "Hola?"

The officer he spoke to in the Zocalo called to give him a report. "We think the kid is named Guzman. Does that ring a bell?"

"Nope. Not at all. Thanks for letting me know. I will see you *manana*. Can you meet me first thing out at *Santa*

Cecila? I want to get a jump on this if we're going to get Salazar back okay."

"What time?" the officer asked.

Mario knew he could get there from his house faster than he could from downtown. "Five in the morning. I meet Benito at six. I want to get you started on it because I know there's evidence there I hope will lead us to Salazar."

"Si, I can be there. The rest of the guys can too I think."

Mario felt more than pleased with the cooperation of all the officers Bene assigned to him. This request would test each of them, and finally prove whether or not they could be trusted. "Can you put out the call for me? I'm dealing with another situation here."

"*Si*. I will see you tomorrow."

"*Gracias*." Mario hung up the phone disappointed.   He hoped they found something out at *Acatitlan* tomorrow, or else the popular priest might not make it home alive.

Twenty Four

Bella Perez stood in the lobby of the Coroner's office waiting to find out more about the man who was gunned down in front of the Cathedral. Fortunately she and her crew were the only ones on the scene. Maybe now she could finally scoop the networks.

After waiting for nearly twenty minutes, a man with thick glasses appeared. "You with the news?"

At least he didn't ask if I'm with CNN. She extended her hand. "*Si*, Bella Perez."

"We notified the next of kin, so you can release the information."

Bella was thrilled. It was probably just one of many gang or drug related crimes, but nevertheless, she would be the first to report it. "*Si, gracias.* Who was he?"

"Tony Guzman."

Bella searched her memory for the name that seemed so familiar to her. "Did you say Guzman?"

He nodded.

"May I?" She peeked over his shoulder, hoping to get inside to see for herself even though she honestly didn't want to see the dead body again. She always hated that part of her job, but bodies always meant better ratings, so she did what she had to.

The man shrugged. "*Si.*" He led her into the ice cold room.

The boy's body lay stretched on a metal gurney. He lowered the sheet so she could see his face.

He looked completely different in death than in life, but once she saw that face, there was no doubt. Tony Guzman. Bella gasped. "I knew him." For the first time in her career, rather than filming the body or clamoring for the scoop, Bella thanked the man, turned around and left. ***

By the time the phone rang in their house, the executive and his wife just finished their bowl of popcorn and were about to go to bed.

"I'll get it dear," he told her. He listened while officers described what happened to his son earlier in the evening.

"We are sorry for your loss, *senor.* We will investigate and bring you answers soon."

The executive quietly hung up the phone. He decided not to bother his wife with this tonight. He didn't want to lose sleep over something he could deal with later. Tomorrow would be bad enough.

***

Father Salazar cracked his eyes open in the middle of the night, shocked and frightened. He couldn't remember where he was or exactly what happened. He stared up at the plain white ceiling, tried to breathe but couldn't. His mouth was stuffed with a tube and taped shut. He didn't feel any pain, but couldn't move a muscle.

Soon it all came flooding back to him – the massacre in the Cathedral, his kidnapping and the giant who threatened him. Only now he wondered how he got here. This must be a hospital. Yes. He had a heart attack and was certain God would call him home. Had the giant shown mercy on him after all? Apparently so. God must have big plans for him, Salazar thought while he drifted back to sleep.

Twenty Five

When Mario reached his mother's neighborhood, he walked around the block first, checking every car to make sure they were safe. From what he could tell, the coast was clear tonight, at least for now. He pulled out his cell and called his mother. "I just got off the metro and I'll be there in a minute. Open up in a few minutes, but not until I get there okay?"

"Si," she replied.

He walked up the hill, through his yard, and knocked on the door. To his dismay, his mother swung it wide open. "Mama, what is wrong with you?"

Elsa wore the same crumpled up t-shirt from the past two days, her hair slightly matted, eyes swollen up. "What?"

"You never open a door in this neighborhood without checking to see who's there first. What did I tell you?"

"I've been living in this same house for over twenty years."

He rolled his eyes. He loved his mother, but she exasperated him at times. "I don't care. It isn't safe." He stepped inside, kissed her cheek. "Where's Sylvia?"

"She's lying down in the back. Oh, Mario. She is so broken. We have too much in common."

Mario walked through the back of his tiny family home and knocked on the bedroom door. He heard the sound of quiet crying. "Sylvia? May I come in?"

"Si." Sylvia lay on her side, crumpled up in a ball on Angela's old childhood bed.

"I am so sorry about Carlos."

"Your mother and I lost our babies. What will we do? How will we go on?"

He wondered how any of them would pick up the pieces of their shattered lives after such tragedy. "I don't know. You have other kids, right?"

"Si, of course, but no one can replace my Carlos."

"No, of course not. I didn't mean it that way. I just wanted to tell you your other kids need to stay away from this house for a few days, that's all."

She wiped her tears. "Why?"

"I don't think it's safe right now."

She sniffed. "I didn't bother to call them yet. I don't know how to tell them they don't have a brother anymore." She broke down in sobs.

Mario felt so bad for her and his mother. "Sylvia, I want to take you and Mama over to my house tonight. It's not a very big place, and I'm not sure how clean it is, but you are welcome to stay in my bed if you want and I will sleep on the—"

"Why would I do that?" Sylvia wiped her eyes on her sleeve.

"Because it is not safe here. I cannot go home tonight and leave the two of you here after what's happened. I only live a few Metro stops up the road. It won't take more than fifteen minutes to get there."

"I'm not going anywhere. This is my home. This is where I live, where Carlos lives...or *lived*." She broke down again.

"No Sylvia, Carlos is no longer here, and neither is my sister. You are next door neighbors and this is part of the same crime. You are not safe and there is no way you will stay here tonight. Get your things. We leave in five minutes, even if I carry you both out of here myself."

***

It was almost midnight when Mario arrived home with his mother and Sylvia in tow. He unlocked the door to his one bedroom flat. The air smelled musky and stale. He opened up the windows and turned on a small fan in the corner. "Sorry about the mess. I haven't been home in awhile."

Elsa cast a disapproving eye on his place, running her finger over the dust marks on his table. "You need a woman in your life."

"Not now, Mama." He carried Sylvia's bags into the back. "You can have the bedroom, Sylvia. Mama, you can have the couch. I will sleep by the door with my gun."

Elsa raised her eyebrows. "Is that necessary?"

Mario sighed. "Don't give me a hard time, okay? I'm protecting you."

His mother mumbled something and went into his kitchen, opened his refrigerator. "Your milk is stale and you don't have any food."

"Aye, aye, aye. Please come out here and get ready for bed, Mama. We have a big day ahead of us tomorrow, *si*?"

"I'm just saying…"

Mario chuckled and put an arm around her shoulder. "*Si*, I told you I haven't been home. Sit down, relax."

Elsa scooted herself across each cushion until she found one without a spring sticking up. "The service for your sister is at two in the afternoon, you know."

"Did you tell Bene?"

His mother scowled. "I called his secretary today, *si*."

"*Bueno*."

Elsa crossed her arms, grumbling under her breath.

"Mama, he loved her. He wants to be there."

"*Si*, I know. He is paying for the service."

"What?"

Elsa nodded. "His secretary insisted."

Mario shrugged. "Well he can afford something nice for her, so if that is what he wants, then so be it."

"He did it because he feels guilty." Elsa said. "Because he knows he killed her."

"He did not kill her."

"Might as well have."

Mario could not disagree. "Regardless, he loved her, so let's just be grateful and think about that, okay?"

"Grateful? About what? My little girl is murdered and nobody can tell me who did it."

There was no easy way to tell his mother what he'd done, but he hoped by doing so, she might feel vindicated. "I killed some of the people responsible."

"You didn't kill them all though, did you? Otherwise Sylvia would still have a son tonight."

Sylvia appeared in the hallway and leaned against the doorjamb. Fresh tears welled up in her eyes.

He couldn't believe his mother's response. She raised him Catholic. *Thou Shalt Not Kill.* Were they all going mad, or worse, going straight to hell? Had the world corrupted them all so much that they didn't respect life anymore than the people who killed his sister and Carlos? It sickened him to think of it. He took a breath, knitted his hands. "Mama, we have company tonight, remember? Please, let's talk about this later."

***

Three men with thick black tattoos arrived at Sylvia Ortiz home in the middle of the night. Surprised to find no one home, they kicked in the door, rummaged through drawers, pulled out the belongings and dumped them in the middle of the living room, knocked over the old TV set in the corner and tipped the furniture upside down, just enough damage to frighten anyone who came home. *And send the proper message.*

Once finished, they went next door and did the same thing to Elsa Martinez' house, tossing a rock through the plate glass window in front, they kicked over her statue of Mother Mary, tore her pictures from the wall, stomping them into the ground, cracking the tube on her TV with a hammer, before dumping it into the floor.

In the kitchen, they knocked over the stacks of bills piled high on the table, scattering them all around the place.

One of the intruders found something of interest and picked it up. Mario Martinez' name on a piece of junk mail. He noticed the address was different than this one. He tucked it away in his jacket pocket. The boss would be pleased.

In the bedroom, he went through the jewelry, pocketing several pieces. This lady had a lot more than the other. He could sell it on the street, make some side cash, all while accomplishing his goal.

One of the men picked up Elsa's phone and made a call. "Hey boss?"

"Do you have any idea what time it is you idiot? I'm in bed."

"Si, I wanted to let you know we tried the two houses you told us to visit tonight, but they are all gone."

"What? You're obviously at the wrong place."

"No, *senor*. Both houses are empty. We missed them, but we messed things up, just like you asked."

"Good. What number are you calling from?"

"The house phone here," he said.

"Idiot. We will deal with this tomorrow. Get out of there. Now."

DAY THREE
July 3

Twenty Six

B y dawn the following morning, hundreds of hand coiled scrolls tied with red velvet ribbon arrived in mailboxes all over Mexico City.
El Templo participants understood to check their mailboxes regularly, but at this extremely early hour, most would not receive their invitation until at least six in the morning or later.

One man named Fraco, or Frac as his friends called him, worked a crack of dawn shift in a local factory. He always checked his mail at 3:30a.m., just before going to work. He liked that about the organization. They planned in advance to always deliver mail early enough so everyone received word about the location in plenty of time.

He heard about the upcoming meeting from some of the other group members who whispered about the other night and the new leader.

Since their mission failed on *Noche Triste*, leaders raised the stakes for everyone to ensure the gods would be pleased.

Frac opened his mailbox that morning at 3:15 a.m and saw the invitation he expected. He carefully slipped the velvet ribbon off, loosened the parchment paper and read the message. As always, it only said five things: date, time, location, attire and special instructions. Today's announcement read:

July 3, 8:00 p.m., Cerro de la Estrella, street clothes, bring at least one used or broken household item

"Hmm," Frac wondered. "That's tonight. Shorter than usual notice." Something was off, but what? He didn't make it to the event on July 1st. He hoped everything worked out okay.

He folded the note neatly into a square and tucked it into the front pocket of his jeans for safekeeping. Tonight he would be there for sure. Before leaving for work, he went inside, dug through the kitchen cabinet looking for the old toaster he broke a few weeks back and put it in the trunk of his car just to make sure he wouldn't forget. Then he finished getting ready for work. He brushed his teeth, shaved the excess stubble from his face and thought about tonight. *Strange for them to request old household items.* He never considered the group charitable before… Maybe they wanted to turn over a new leaf.

***

Jerry Montoya worked from his home office the following morning. His day job as an investment banker proved quite demanding, but he'd taken the past week off and still had one more week of vacation to go before heading back to his office in the *Bolsa Mexicana de Valores*, or BMV, also known as the Mexican Stock Exchange.

He studied the stock market in the daily paper, making notes, contemplating his own portfolio when his telephone rang. "Hola."

"Montoya?"

"*Si.*"

"You did us a great service yesterday."

"*Gracias, senor.*"

"Do you know why I'm calling?"

Montoya leaned back in his leather chair, took off his reading glasses. Actually, he had an idea, but didn't want to jinx anything. "No."

The caller laughed. "Dennis, I hope you know your work for El Templo is not only important, but recognized. Not only yesterday, but many other times, your direct involvement in our operations has been key to our success. I presume you heard what happened on *Noche Triste, si*?"

"Si, but I missed that evening."

"You know we meet tonight and are currently without a leader…"

Montoya's heart raced, his palms got a bit sweaty. "Uh huh."

"Well? What do you say? Will you assume the role for us, starting tonight?"

To actually hear the words of acknowledgement Montoya prayed for these past several years seemed like a dream. He always knew if he kept his faith, did his part, then maybe, just maybe, he would eventually receive the recognition he richly deserved. Still, this moment seemed surreal. "Of course I will."

"*Magnifico.* We meet tonight at 8:00 p.m. *Cerro de la Estrella.*"

The location confused Montoya. *Cerro de la Estrella* was an ancient Aztec temple site located right in the heart of Mexico City near Districto Federal. "Isn't that too out in the open for our purposes?"

The caller laughed. "Montoya, since when are we concerned about that?"

"I just thought…since things didn't go as planned the other night…"

"No sacrifice will occur out in the open. We will gather there first before moving to the sacred location. You will lead them. Tonight is the New Fire Ceremony. We gave shorter than normal notice for our protection and once they arrive, you will remind everyone of their vows and lead them to the ritual site. *Comprende?*"

Montoya studied the requirements of the New Fire Ceremony, but he realized he would need further study to prepare for his words tonight. For now, he would keep his questions to himself. "*Si* I understand. What will I wear tonight, Your Eminence? My traditional costume and masks are not in alignment with my new role."

"Due to our discretionary measures, you will wear only your black hood and mask with street clothes for tonight. Once we disclose the location of the sacrifice, you will change into full regalia, *comprende?*"

Montoya felt better knowing he could arrive in his normal clothing. "*Si.*"

"Until tonight, then. Oh, and don't forget to bring a used household item."

Montoya hated to admit he didn't know why he needed anything from his house, but he chose not to ask why or mention it at the moment. "*Si, gracias, Senor.* I do not take this honor lightly."

"You shouldn't." The line went dead.

For his own safety and for the sanctity of his new position, Montoya recognized the need for his identity to remain hidden from the masses. He closed his newspaper and went to find the appropriate books and wardrobe for tonight which would prove one of the most important moments of his entire life.

Twenty Seven

After making his mother and Sylvia promise to stay put in his house until he could come get them for the funeral that afternoon, Mario arrived at *Santa Cecilia Acatitlan* temple around 4:45a.m. the following morning.

He brought his own flashlight and containers for specimens, expecting to be alone so early and shocked when he found all ten men already there waiting for him. "*Buenos dias* everyone. *Muchos gracias* for coming out so early."

"We agree we need to get a head start on this today," one of them said.

He led them inside the interior of the main temple and showed them where he found the blood evidence the night Benito almost got sacrificed, "In here," he pointed to the inner chamber. "See?" Sure enough, flashlights revealed the caked on blood and trace samples of feathers and other items.

Half of the men followed Mario outside the gate. Although the trash he saw the other day blew away or disappeared, he knew there must be more evidence out here somewhere. "When I investigated this site, it looked like the carnival just left town. I want you to pull footprints, lint, dust, trash, anything with useable DNA samples. Also check for blood or anything suspicious and search all the way out to those houses and the museum." He pointed to the farthest fence where cars parked during events. "Any questions?"

They shook their heads.

"Call my cell if you need me, *si*?"

They nodded.

"*Bueno.* I have a meeting downtown, but I'll be back as soon as I can. If you find anything important, give me a call. Thank you for your time this morning."

***

Mario stepped off the Metro and ran toward the Palacio at the crack of dawn. So distracted and concerned about being late for his meeting with Bene, he never even saw the black car with tinted windows coming straight toward him, until he heard the sound of gunshots.

"Get down," someone shouted at him.

He dove to the pavement, landing behind a concrete barricade. A car screeched around the corner and out of sight. His heart raced. He pushed himself up, rubbed the side of his head where a knot started to form.

A man ran over and helped him up. "Hey, are you okay?"

Mario couldn't speak. He braced himself on the man and stood. "*Si, gracias.*" He stumbled toward the Palacio.

Several uniformed Presidential guards and policia ran up to him with their guns drawn. "Are you okay?"

He didn't know how to answer. Someone tried to kill him. He wasn't quite sure what to think. "*Si*."

"Did you happen to see the plates on the car?" an officer asked.

"No, it happened so fast."

"We will take a look at the video surveillance tapes, see if we can make an ID.," another officer said. "Meanwhile, you sure you're okay?"

"*Si*. I'm meeting with *El Presidente*. I can't be late."

"Of course," the officer said.

He thanked the man who helped him and followed the police up the stairs and inside the Palacio. Pulse still elevated, Mario finally caught his breath about the time they stepped into the building.

Bene rushed up to Mario as soon as he stepped in the office. "Are you okay? I heard someone shot at you."

"How did you hear about that? It just happened." Mario laughed and tried to make a joke.

Benito wasn't amused. "This isn't funny. I want to know you're okay."

Mario rubbed his head. "*Si,* I'm fine. I'm pretty sure it's the same car I saw yesterday."

"Someone removed the plates from the car."

"What? How did you find that out?"

"My security team films and guards everything around the clock."

"Can they pull the tapes from yesterday and at least make sure it's the same car?" Mario asked. "Maybe they could zoom in on the driver…"

"Unfortunately we only use video surveillance around the Palacio, not around the Cathedral Metropolitano," Bene said.

"Too bad. Did they film the other night too?"

"I know what you're thinking, and yes, but the trouble is the suspects covered themselves with masks and face paint. We couldn't ID any of them."

Rita brought Mario an ice pack and a towel. "Are you okay? Here let me get that for you." She pressed the ice pack to his head. "There. Keep the ice on it."

"*Gracias*, Rita. It feels better already."

"Good. You let me know if you need anything else," Rita said.

"Rita, why don't you get us some coffee and some pastries?" Bene asked.

"Right away."

"Rita's likes to mother anyone and everyone she can," Bene said.

"Si, my mother is like that also."

"Angela told me all about your mother..." Bene got a far off look in his eye. "I can't believe her funeral is today. God how I wish I married her."

Mario cleared his throat and fought off tears. With all that happened the past few days, he easily pushed thoughts of his sister from his mind, but this afternoon, his grief would be unavoidable.

Bene noticed his silence. "I'm sorry. I can't help thinking about her."

He needed to change the subject. "Something happened you need to know."

Bene sighed. "Come and sit."

Mario took his now familiar seat at the Presidente's table. "Carlos is dead, Bene. They got to him."

Benito's mouth fell open. "Oh no…"

"Si, and Salazar is still missing, the other kid was shot and killed, and now this shooting today…"

"I don't know what we're going to do," Bene said.

Mario suddenly remembered the photo he took with his cell. "Oh. I need to show you something, too." He pulled out the phone, scrolled to the appropriate screen and held it up for Bene to see. "You know him?"

Bene studied the photo of the dead young man on the Cathedral steps. "This is him?"

Mario stared at the table, while Rita walked in and brought their breakfast. "Si."

"This is horrible." Bene said.

"I take it that means you don't recognize him?"

Bene shook his head and started to hand the phone back to Mario just as his father walked in.

"Good morning," Juarez Senior said. "What did I miss?"

Twenty Eight

Elsa felt antsy. Although Mario pleaded with her and Sylvia to stay at his house until he could come get them for the funeral, she couldn't do it. Her son's place looked like a train wreck, and he had no food whatsoever anywhere in the house.

He offered to buy groceries for them before going to work this morning, but how could she allow him to do that when he had so much else on his mind?

She wandered through his tiny one bedroom home, picking up his scattered laundry, doing some dishes, taking out the trash that piled up for weeks on end. It didn't take long, and once she finished, Elsa wanted to go home.

Sylvia slept in late, which was a good thing after all she'd been through yesterday. She appeared in the kitchen doorway right about the time Elsa finished washing the last plate in the sink. "*Buenos dias*."

Elsa wiped her hands and threw the dishtowel over the cupboard door. "*Hola*." She walked up, hugged her friend. "How are you feeling today?"

Sylvia's eyes watered immediately. "I'm not sure."

"*Si*, I understand. I don't think my son left us any food here. Want to go home?"

Sylvia nodded.

"Good. Go take a shower if you want to, then we can catch the metro."

"I'm ready now," Sylvia said. "I'll get my things."

Elsa felt relieved. Angela's funeral started in a few hours and she needed to make sure she looked her best. She went into the living room and sat on the couch near the door and waited.

***

Senora Sanchez showed up to work earlier than usual the following morning half expecting to find Dennis Montoya sitting in her desk where he spent much of the past week. Today, her office was empty, which made her even more upset.

Nothing seemed right with Dennis lately, and although she couldn't put her finger on it, she had a bad feeling it had something to do with Mario Martinez' sister. She had no evidence, no proof, but the way he treated Mario seemed unnatural and from the way he'd been acting, Montoya was hiding something.

She wondered if she should call Mario, arrange to meet him somewhere to tell him her suspicions. He might think she was paranoid, but what if her intuition was right? If anyone else got killed, or if Father Salazar died and she found out later Montoya had anything to do with it, she could never forgive herself.

Then again, her instincts told her to keep clear of a dangerous situation for her own good. She would think about it awhile longer before making up her mind. If she didn't hear of a break in the case in the newspaper in the next twenty four hours, she would say something, if not, she would keep her suspicions to herself.

Sanchez sifted through the stacks of papers Montoya left on her desk. It irked her that the man chose to make a mess of everything here. If he wanted to use her phone, that was one thing, but to leave everything in such disarray was another. She sifted through the papers, tossing them aside. Most looked like mindless scribbling. Half way through the mess, though, a business card slipped out on the floor. Sanchez studied the name. It seemed familiar. She flipped it over and saw a strange hand drawn symbol on the back. She recognized it as one featured prominently in her Museo and conducted a quick search in her database of artifact photos.

She scrolled through the list of various ancient symbols until she found it, enlarged it and gasped: *Death and War*

Why would Montoya draw something like this? She picked up the phone and dialed Mario's cell. No answer. She would try again later.

Twenty Nine

When Juarez Senior walked into Benito's office, Mario and Bene instantly burst out laughing. With nothing even remotely funny about anything in their lives, the way he asked what he'd missed since Mario was nearly gunned down in the streets seemed like the funniest thing in the world.

"What are you two laughing at?" Juarez Senior demanded. "You act like a couple of immature school boys."

"Papa," Bene bent over and tried to stop. "You should have been here, right Mario?"

Mario's eyes watered from laughter for the first time in a long time. He leaned over to calm his aching stomach muscles, tight from laughing so hard, and rubbed his head with the ice pack. "Ouch." He continued laughing. "Stop Bene. You're making my head hurt."

Juarez Senior's face twisted into an annoyed scowl, which made them laugh all the harder. "Are you making fun of me?"

Rita sat a hot pot of coffee in the center of the table and chuckled herself. "No, *Senor* Juarez. It's been quite a morning so far, that's all."

"Oh…" Bene leaned back in his chair and tried to catch his breath. "I needed that. Thank you, father."

"Si, me too," Mario smiled.

"Will the two of you knock it off and tell me what's going on around here?" Juarez Senior asked.

Bene still laughed a bit. "Well Father, if you're asking if Mario okay after someone tried to gun him down outside the Palacio this morning then the answer is yes. He's fine."

They both burst out in a fresh wave of laughter.

"Stop!" Juarez shouted. He appeared genuinely shocked. "What are you talking about?"

Mario slapped his hand on his knee and kept right on laughing. He couldn't stop to save his life. "Stop Bene. Please. This is not showing respect to your father."

"Are you serious?" Juarez Senior asked.

Rita peeked in the door. "*Si, senor*. Mario had a close call this morning."

"Then what is so funny?"

Benito snickered. "*Nada*."

Mario sucked in air and calmed down. "You're right, *Senor* Juarez. Nothing here is funny. I think we are both so stressed out, we needed a good laugh. It beats the alternative."

Bene briefly explained to his father what happened earlier. "And Mario was just showing me a photo of the young man who was shot last night." He reached across the table and picked up Mario's cell, handed it to his father.

"Oh no," Juarez Senior said.

"What?"

"I know this young man. This is Guzman's son."

Bene's mouth fell open. "You mean the Guzman from TelMex?"

Juarez Senior brought his hand to his mouth. "*Si.*"

Mario and Bene gave each other a knowing look, but kept their other thoughts to themselves as the room filled with laughter only moments ago became deathly silent.

Thirty

"From now on, Mario cannot leave this office without some kind of formal protection," Juarez Senor insisted.

Bene agreed. "Rita will assign you a bulletproof vest."

He stared out the window into the Zocalo still running the shooting over in his mind. He tried to remember the car, but didn't pay attention to anything but getting to the Palacio. From now on, he needed to be more careful, look over his shoulder and make sure things were clear.

"Mario?" Bene asked. "Did you hear me?"

He turned around. "Sorry. I'm a million miles away."

"I can see that. I said I want to give you a bulletproof vest to wear at all times."

Mario scowled. "Is that really necessary?" As soon as the words came out of his mouth, he remembered his mother questioning him about the gun. Bene did this for his protection and he would gladly accept.

Bene nodded.

"You don't think Guzman's boy had anything to do with your kidnapping or Salazar, do you?" Juarez Senior asked.

Bene shrugged. "We don't know, father."

Mario quickly lost his patience. "Listen, speaking of Salazar, I left the men out at Santa Cecelia. I need to get back and see if they uncovered anything. We still don't have any good leads on Father Salazar. If you want me to wear a vest, fine, but I need to go. I need to go pick up my mother for the funeral."

"Hang on, Mario, just a minute." Bene called Rita at her desk and told her what he wanted. "Rita has a protective vest in the outer closet I think should fit you. I want you to put it on right now. If you need help figuring it out how to put it on…"

"I think I can manage," Mario smiled.

"Wear it at all times," Bene said. "Promise."

"I promise, only if you wear one too. You and your father, even Rita, we all need protection. Oh and one more thing."

"What?" Bene asked.

"Especially after what went on this morning, I'm not sure you should go to the funeral today. I'm not sure it's safe."

Bene swallowed hard, his eyes welled up. "I loved Angela with all my heart. I have to go. I've tried not to think too much about her, because I'm afraid if I did, I would not want to live, and I know the people need me to stay here and fight for them. That is the only thing keeping me together right now."

Mario nodded. "I agree."

"I'm going to Angela's funeral today."

Mario sighed. "I am not sure this is a good idea. We don't know who is after us right now and the situation isn't contained yet."

"Good idea or not, I don't care," Bene stood up and slapped Mario on the back. "Now let's get you fitted for that vest. Also, I'm going to send a car for you and your family today. Give me the address. I don't want any of you driving on your own to Angela's service, particularly under the circumstances."

Nobody in Mario's family had a car. They would have taken the Metro. "Thank you, Bene."

"That's what brothers are for."

***

Once properly suited up in his new vest, Mario left the Palacio and just reached the Zocalo when his cell rang. "Hola?"

"It's *Senora* Sanchez. I need to see you right away."

Although he had a million other things to do, the sound of her voice caught his attention, "Is everything okay?"

She hesitated, then said, "I...I'm not sure. There's something here I want you to see."

Good, maybe a crack in the case. "I'll be right there."

Thirty One

The video surveillance supervisor for Juarez Hospital stood outside his employee's office. The cramped space was stuffed floor to ceiling with used tapes, stacks of files and other odds and ends. "I need you to look up something for me."

The on-duty security officer Jose had his crunched potato chips. He wiped his hands on his pant legs and took the tape from his boss. "Why what's up?"

"A John Doe came in late yesterday afternoon. Billing wants to know who he is."

The kid was busy watching television at the moment. "Uh huh."

His boss walked over and pulled his headphones out of his ears. "That means now."

Jose seemed taken aback. "Alright. Just a minute."

His boss scowled. "Hurry up. Billing needs to know who's paying for his open heart surgery."

He took his feet off the desk and pulled his chair forward to the control panels. "What time did he come in?"

"Around four yesterday afternoon."

Jose pulled up the files, rolled the video back and fast forwarded through the shots of yesterday afternoon. "There he is."

A huge young man dragged a victim through the hospital lobby, leaned the ill man against the trashcan and called out for help. Not a big deal. Strangers dropped people off all the time, but if either could be identified, billing would want to know.

Jose slowed down the video and noticed a tattoo on the Good Samaritan's hand. He also noticed the unmistakable ring around his neck. "Hey." he told his boss. "I think I know that guy."

At that moment, a news story flashed on the television screen with the words BREAKING NEWS. The sexy news reporter Bella Perez stood outside the Cathedral next to a dead body, and a recent photo of the victim.

Jose unplugged his earphones from the television set so his boss could hear too.

The victim's face flashed on screen. His name: Tony Guzman

Jose pointed to the TV. "Hey. Look. It's the same guy."

The supervisor glanced on the TV screen and back at the monitor. "Are you sure?"

"Positive. Look at the clothes, the hair, the tattoo ring on the neck."

The supervisor squinted at the video camera and back to the photo on the TV screen. "I think you're right."

"I know I'm right," Jose grabbed for his chip bag again. "This is for real, *senor*."

"Looks like we've got quite a situation on our hands."

Jose raised his eyebrows. "I'll call Bella Perez. She'll love this story." And he would love checking her out in the meantime.

"Wait just a minute. Before you go calling the TV people, take another look and make sure."

The victim's photo flashed on the screen again, along with a telephone number to call with any leads on the case. Then the camera panned back to Bella, who stood next to the dead body. "That's him. I know it. Look at his clothes. They're the same." Sure enough, he wore the same too baggy jeans and black hooded shirt. Apparently Tony Guzman, the Good Samaritan, was dead.

"We better call it in."

Jose reached for the phone.

"No," the supervisor picked up the phone himself. "I'll do it. You get back to work."

Jose rolled his eyes. "Whatever. Just make sure you ask for Bella."

***

Bella stood outside the Palacio. Her cameraman zoomed in on the fresh bullet marks in the concrete barriers. "Are you getting it?" She pointed out the holes to Pedro, just in case.

Pedro mumbled. "Si."

She turned around to find the perfect spot to stand where the camera had a full shot of her new dress and the damage, when she saw Mario Martinez running out of the Palacio. "Hey Mario."

He waved to her, but kept on running.

Bella took off after him, catching him right outside the doors to the Templo Mayor. "Wait up."

He spun around. "Bella, Not now. Can I catch you later?"

She didn't get where she was by being polite. "Question. Did you see who got shot at this morning in the Zocalo?" She held her mic up to his mouth.

Pedro ran with his camera to catch up.

Mario scowled. "Listen. Even if I did know who got shot at today, which I don't, I would not tell you with him…" He pointed right at Pedro. "…pointing that stupid camera in my face. You seem like a nice person, Bella, but I can't do this now. I've gotta go." He disappeared into the door of the Museo.

She spun around. "Is the tape rolling?"

Pedro nodded.

"Three two one, There you have it, ladies and gentlemen, the Presidente's new best friend officially saying he does not know the victim in the latest shooting in the Zocalo. Are citizens safe? Only time will tell, meanwhile, I'm Bella Perez, bringing you the very latest on this story as it develops."

She turned off her mic, cinched her bra a little tighter and smiled. "Pretty good, huh?"

"Uh huh," Pedro checked the monitor. "Good."

Thirty Two

Elsa Martinez and Sylvia Ortiz got off the Metro and walked a few blocks up the hill to their respective homes.

"I will meet you outside at one thirty for the service." Sylvia stood in Elsa's yard, hesitated slightly, obviously scared to be alone. "Thanks for everything."

Elsa smiled and took her hand. "Everything will work out in time, you know. We will get through this together."

Sylvia's eyes watered. "*Si.*"

"Now go on and get ready and I will see you in just a bit. Knock if you need anything." Elsa turned and screamed when she saw broken glass on the ground. "Agh. Someone broke in."

Sylvia came running. "Oh no. What should we do?"

Elsa immediately went straight to the open front door and stepped into her living room. Her heart nearly broke at the sight of the treasures collected over a lifetime now shattered in a thousand pieces in the floor. The twisted remains of Angela's high school picture lay in the center of the room. She bent down picked up the dented frame, dusting shards of glass off of Angela's face and cutting herself in the process, before opening the photo up and sitting it back where it belonged. "I can't believe this. Who would do such a terrible thing?"

Sylvia's hands trembled as she picked up one of Elsa's throw pillows off the floor. "I don't know. What should we do? Call the policia?"

Elsa shook her head. "No, not until Mario gets here. He doesn't like me calling policia without him around. I better clean it up before I tell him. He won't like this at all."

"Si, I will help you," Sylvia started to gather things up in piles.

"You don't need to," Elsa smiled through her tears.

"We would get through this together," Sylvia said. "And that is exactly what we'll do."

Elsa stepped inside the kitchen and noticed her phone off the hook and papers scattered all around. "I don't even know where to begin."

***

A half hour later, Elsa and Sylvia had the mess pretty well cleaned up, with the exception of the vacant spot where the front window used to be.

Elsa sat on the couch, chin in hands and surveyed their progress. Within a few hours she would bury her daughter, and afterward, she planned to host her entire family here. The place didn't look perfect, but she figured it would do. "Thank you for helping me, Sylvia."

Sylvia took a seat beside her. "Of course. I can help you cook today too. It will help get my mind off of…"

Elsa picked Angela's broken photo up and clutched it to her heart. "I will help you cook soon too."

Sylvia walked to the front door, which gaped open. She stared out into the yard as the heat of the day started to settle in to the living room. "I can't think about Carlos today or I won't have the strength to help you. I will think of him *manana*."

"*Si*, I understand." Elsa stood and took another look around the living room. "This looks better, huh?"

"Si, but I see some bigger glass pieces still in the yard. Let me run home and get a bigger broom and I can help you with that also."

"*Gracias*," Elsa said. "I should call Mario and tell him what happened." Elsa went to the kitchen, picked up the phone and dialed. Nobody answered. She didn't want to scare him by leaving a message about what happened, so she hung up. She put the phone back in the cradle once she heard Sylvia screaming and ran outside.

Sylvia ran across the yard, waving her arms, crying. "Elsa. They got my place too."

Elsa got the chills. "Oh my God. What is happening to us? On second thought, we better call Mario."

Thirty Three

Senora Sanchez paced around her office wondering if she did the right thing trusting Mario, but if *El Presidente* confided in him, she believed it would be okay.

Someone knocked. "Senora Sanchez?" Mario stood in her doorway.

"Yes?"

"What do you need?" His cell rang and he glanced at it.

"Thanks for coming. Do you need to get that?"

He shook his head. "Oh, no, that's my mother. I will call her back in a minute."

Sanchez gulped. "Come in, take a seat." She went around to the back of her desk and fumbled through the papers Montoya left on her desk.

Mario scowled. "What's wrong? You didn't sound well on the phone."

Sanchez stared at her hands, clicked her new manicured nails together. "What I want to discuss must remain between you and me. Can you promise me?"

"Not if it has something to do with Father Salazar. I don't have a single lead yet, other than my belief someone held against his will underneath your Museo. I am hoping you called me here with some new information to help me find him. I never make promises I can't keep."

Sanchez nodded. At least he was honest, but it wasn't what she wanted to hear. "I understand. I just meant…I believe something dangerous is happening around here."

"Oh?" He laughed. "And when did you finally figure that out? My sister's mutilated body didn't convince you, huh?"

"Mario—"

He sighed. "No Senora. You've given me a hard time about this investigation from the very beginning, so why don't you tell me what you want so I can get on with my day? I have a missing person to find and a funeral to attend."

Sanchez couldn't blame Mario for hating her right now. She'd been nothing short of horrible to him. "I'm sorry, but I thought you should see this." She slid the business card across her desk, with the drawing face up.

He laughed. "You called me over here for this? What is this? Some stupid kid's drawing?"

"No, it's a symbol."

"What kind?"

"Aztec. It means Death, War."

Mario rolled his eyes and turned the card over. Something caught his attention. "Who did this belong to?"

"Senor Montoya. The card fell out of some of his other notes he left in my office. I found the card while I cleaned his things out early this morning, and thought it might be important."

"Do you know this man?" He flipped the business card over so Sanchez could read the name on it.

She shook her head. "No."

Mario held it closer, stood up from his chair and shouted, "Are you sure?"

She shrugged. "Yes."

"Antonio Guzman, *Presidente of TelMex*. You're saying you don't know him? You've never met him, even in this prestigious position?"

Sanchez flinched, tears formed in her eyes. "No, I swear."

He pounded his palm on her desk. "You better hope you don't, *Senora* Sanchez." He snapped the card up from her desk, slipped it in his pocket. "I'm taking this as evidence. Now goodbye. I have a kidnapping to solve." He slammed the door behind him.

Sanchez cried and her hands trembled. She picked up the papers Mario knocked over and started neatly stacking them back on her desk. She did the right thing, she told herself. That symbol meant something. Mario would figure it out, and with any kind of luck, nobody would find out she had anything to do with it.

***

The executive Antonio Guzman, Presidente of TelMex, the largest telephone service provider in Mexico, left his office and walked across the Plaza de la Constitution on his way to meet a business associate for lunch.

A man in a black leather jacket approached. "Senor."

Guzman scowled. "I told you never to approach me in broad daylight. Now if you'll excuse me, I am meeting someone." He tried to push past the man.

He blocked Guzman's passage, grabbed him by the forearm. "Excuse me, but I have a message for you from The Great One."

Guzman growled. "If you don't get your hands off me right now, you'll be more than sorry."

"The One wanted me to remind you that you were warned about bringing family into the business."

"What do you know about fam—" Before Guzman finished, several bullets silently penetrated his gut. His eyes wide with shock, blood gurgled from his mouth. He stared his assailant in the eye and fell.

"Consider yourself warned," the man turned away. "Have a nice day."

Guzman fell forward on the ground and dropped dead on the spot.

The man in the black leather jacket disappeared before anyone noticed.

***

Bella and Pedro walked back to the van to follow up on a lead at Juarez Hospital when they heard someone cry out from across *Plaza de la Constitution*.

"Help. Someone help. A man's been shot."

Bella squinted into the sun and saw a man in a suit on his knees helping another businessman lying on the ground. "Quick Pedro. Get the camera rolling." She kicked off her heels and ran across the square. "It looks like I'm finally going to get the break I've been waiting for."

Thirty Four

Mario could hardly believe the coincidence of finding Guzman's business card in Montoya's belongings. It figured. He knew Montoya was a worm, now he had proof.

He stepped out the front door of the Museo and into the busy Zocalo and immediately noticed the commotion in front of the Palacio. Adrenaline shot through his veins and he instinctively ran toward the crowd.

At least twenty policia descended in the center of the Plaza de la Constitucion, right in front of the Palacio, along with a TV truck, and from the looks of it, they did their best to block the area off and keep the public away from whatever happened. Whatever it was, it couldn't be good.

Mario reached the other side of the square and pushed his way through the growing crowd, trying to get close before the Policia stopped him.

A tall officer with a big gun stepped forward and pressed his palm on Mario's shoulder. "That's far enough, sir. We have a situation here and I'm afraid you need to stand back."

He backed down and reached for his wallet. "My name is Martinez. I work for *El Presidente*." He flashed his regular government ID, not knowing if it would work, but in this case, he got lucky.

Recognition flashed across the officer's face and he nodded. "Oh *si*. I saw you on TV yesterday with *El Presidente*."

"Si, that was me," Mario smiled.

The officer lifted the yellow police tape back and gestured him forward. "Come on in."

Behind the police lines, five officers kneeled next to some medics. Mario moved past them to get a closer look at the scene. A distinguished looking gentleman in a dark grey business suit, probably in his mid to late fifties laid face first in the street in a large pool of blood. Judging from the lack of response from the medical team, Mario knew he was dead. He tapped one of the officers on the shoulder. "Excuse me, who is it?"

"Antonio Guzman," the officer whispered. "You know, the head of *TelMex*?"

Mario got a cold chill. "Oh *si*, I know him."

"Mario."

Mario heard the sound of the annoyingly familiar voice, and sure enough, he left the barricade and saw Bella Perez, now clad in an ice blue skintight business suit. His eyes wandered down her legs and her bare feet. "Yes?"

She awkwardly tried to step on her toes so he might not notice. "I ran to catch the story."

Mario raised his eyebrows. "I see, and did you actually get a story this time? Or I should say a *truthful one*?"

Bella became surprisingly emotional for someone so caddy. Her eyes fell toward the hot cement and her eyes actually filled with tears. "Si."

"What's wrong? What is it?" Mario reached out for her shoulder, looking up to make sure her cameraman wasn't about to deck him.

"Sorry." She sniffed and wiped the mascara from the corners of her eyes. "The family…they were friends of mine. We went to school together."

"You and Tony Guzman?" Mario asked.

"Hey." Bella scowled. "I thought you said you didn't know about any shooting victims."

"You asked me about today, you never said a word about yesterday."

She nodded. "Tony was a good guy."

"How well did you know him?"

She wouldn't answer at first, cleared her throat. "We dated back in high school."

"Oh? Long time?"

She shrugged. "Two years."

"I'm sorry, Bella."

"Don't worry about it. I hadn't seen him in a long time anyhow."

"Do you happen to know what kind of things he was involved in?"

"If you're asking me if I know who killed him and his father, the answer is no. I have no clue. If I did, don't you think I'd report on it?" she snapped.

Mario held his hands up in surrender, as he was prone to do in her hotheaded company. "Hey, I'm just asking. I want to find the people who did this and see if it's related at all to what happened the other night in the Cathedral, that's all."

"And this morning?" She gave him a strange look.

"What about it?"

She smirked. "Pedro happened to catch the whole thing on tape, including the drive by shooting this morning. We did see the man who got shot at earlier today, just in case you wondered."

Mario rolled his eyes. For a ditz the woman knew her stuff. "So? What do you want?"

She batted her eyes. "Nothing."

"You're not going to get a scoop from me, sister, so you may as well keep on digging," he snapped.

She leaned over so he caught a glimpse of her cleavage. "I didn't think you'd mind sharing why someone tried to kill you."

"Seriously, we are trying to solve a crime here and we would appreciate it if you could keep that tape off the news. Do you even understand about the delicate nature of police work, Bella, and how the media compromises our information by spreading half truths and misinformation to the public?"

Bella put her hand on her hip. "Honey, there ain't nothin' misinformed about information caught on film. The camera never lies."

Mario did a once over of Bella's lips, her glossy hair and smooth skin. He knew for sure the camera lied all the time. The truth - Bella was far better looking in person.

***

Bella smiled. In the short time she'd know Mario
Martinez, she'd never known him to be tongue tied until
this very moment. "Well?"

"Well what?"

"Well what do you say to that?" She pursed her lips in a
way she knew drove most men wild.

"That's just it, Bella. I can't make you keep that tape
off the air tonight. I have no control of you whatsoever.
It's up to you. You use your own judgment, but realize that
if you compromise our investigation into the death of Tony
and his father because you chose to air footage of things
you really don't understand, then you have only yourself to
blame and you will be the one who has to live with the
consequences, *comprende*? Now I need to get going, so
I'll see you later." Without another word, Mario turned and
jogged across the Zocalo.

She watched him go. Bella wondered what it would
take to hook a man like Mario. He didn't seem to notice
her at all. "How's my lipstick, Pedro?"

"*Bueno*." He smiled and nodded at her.

Thirty Five

B y the time Mario got away from the annoying
Bella and made it to the subway, he realized
unfortunately, there would not be enough time
today to get back out to Santa Cecilia before the funeral.
Maybe later this afternoon. He hoped the officers found

what they needed and could get any evidence processed quickly, but for now, he needed to head home.

He took a seat and thought about Bella. He hoped she would be able to give him some information about the Guzman's but from the looks of things, she was just that – all looks and little else. His cell rang for the fifth time. His mother called again. "Mama. Hola. What is it?"

"Please Mario. Hurry. We need you."

"Si Mama. I'm almost there now."

"You are?" Elsa sounded surprised.

"Si, I'm on the subway. Hold still and I will be there in a few minutes."

***

Fifteen minutes later, Mario got off the Metro and walked a short distance to his house. He unlocked the door, looked around, but to his surprise, nobody was home. *That's strange.* "Mama?" he called, but still no one answered.

Panic filled him. *What if? No. He had to stay positive. Maybe they went out in the yard, gone to the store…* He searched his bedroom and bathroom and noticed his mother and Sylvia and all their belongings were nowhere to be found. He checked at his cell again, at the caller ID and finally noticed his mother hadn't been calling from here at all, but from her own house. He dialed and before she could finish saying hello, he yelled. "Mama. Where are you and why didn't you wait for me at my house like I told you to?"

Elsa's voice sounded shaky. "Mario. Come quick. Someone broke into both our homes. We don't know what to do. We cleaned some of it up, but…"

His worse fears were becoming reality. If anything happened to his mother, Mario wouldn't have anyone left in the world. "Are the doors secure?"

"No."

He felt the familiar sting of adrenaline shoot through his gut. "Neither place is secure?"

"Sylvia's probably is. Our front window is broken out."

He growled. "My God, Mama. Why don't you listen to me? I told you to stay at my house."

"Sorry, we just thought…"

"No, you didn't think." He sighed with exasperation. He could call the policia, but still didn't trust them completely. He'd never felt more helpless in his life. "Go to Sylvia's house, stay there and lock all the doors until I get there, okay? I should be there in fifteen or twenty minutes. Promise me you will stay in that house and you will not open that door until I call you?"

"Si. Just get here soon."

"Good and stop cleaning. You're destroying evidence." He jotted down Sylvia's number. "I am on my way." He loved his mother more than anything, but sometimes, she irked him beyond belief. She would never listen to a thing he told her.   He planned to take his mother and Sylvia back home and take his time getting ready, but no. *Women.* He could never understand anything they did. He went to his closet and sifted through the hangars until he reached a few items covered in plastic in the far back corner. He grabbed his only suit, his only tie and the only decent pair of slacks he had to his name.

He unwrapped them and hoped they were suitable for this somber occasion. He wasn't sure anything was good enough to honor his sister, but this was the best he had. He wrapped it up again, hung it over his arm, made sure all the doors and windows were locked up and left. Outside he stopped, turned around and went back to get something he forgot. He hoped it was still there.

The heart necklace he gave to Angela years ago lay in the center of the mantle. The policia checked it along with the other evidence, but soon returned it to Mario, saying they couldn't find any new prints or DNA on it. Today, he would give it to someone else. He put it in his pocket, ran out the door and went to catch the train to his mother's house.

***

Minutes after Mario disappeared around the corner to catch the Metro, a black car with tinted windows pulled up in front of his tiny home. The window lowered and a gloved hand reached for his mailbox, taping a letter to it, then blowing hundreds of rounds of ammo through the front windows, doors and walls with an automatic weapon.

The car sped away before anyone came out of their homes or noticed.

Message delivered.

***

The day after his open heart surgery, Father Salazar felt horrible. His incision produced such horrible pain partially due to his advanced age, he slept most of the day, despite repeated attempts to get him up and walking around.

Finally in the afternoon, he opened his eyes. The drugs wore off for the most part, and although he was unable to move much, he wished someone would talk to him so he could tell them who he was and get back to the rectory where he belonged.

Sister Hernandez and the rest of the faithful nuns who served at the Cathedral must be worried sick about him by now. He leaned his head to the right and noticed the telephone. *Oh good.* He would call Sister Hernandez right now and clear all of this up.

He reached his bruised arm out from under his sheet and blanket and stretched it over his bed railing, missing it by mere millimeters. He cringed in pain, but managed to lean out slightly and grabbed the phone, pulling the receiver into his bed. He glanced at the numbers. Rarely if ever did he use a phone, he never needed to. He spent almost all his time at the church. He thought about it for a moment, and started to dial.

The phone rang twice when a tall man in a black leather jacket came into his room, "Need to call someone?" He smiled and pushed the button to hang it up.

Salazar reached his arms out to the man. "Oh good, *si*, maybe you can help me. I need to get a hold of my church, let them know I'm alright."

"You are Father Salazar, aren't you?"

"*Si, si.*" His parched lips smiled and his heart filled with hope.

The man laughed. "Wonderful."

"I'm so glad you're here. I need to get back to my Cathedral before anyone worries."

He chuckled. "I believe there are many people wondering where you are this fine day, Father."

Before Father Salazar could respond, the man pressed a cloth over his mouth and nose. The priest panicked, his eyes widened and he stared into the face of his assailant, breathed in the pungent scent, and lost consciousness.

Thirty Six

Mario panicked the entire way back to his mother's house. He called Rita on the way to make sure Bene knew the correct address to send the car for the funeral.

By the time he reached the end of his street it was nearly one thirty. Benito's car would be at his mother's house any minute now. His pulse quickened as he saw shards of broken glass covering the cactuses and shrubs underneath his mother's window. His breath caught in his throat and he choked up thinking about what he would do if anything happened to either Elsa or Sylvia. He knocked on Sylvia's door.

"Who's there?" she asked.

He was impressed she asked him to identify himself. "It's Mario."

The door opened slowly and a frightened Sylvia peeked out. "Thank God you're here."

He stepped into the living area of her home. He never saw inside Sylvia's house before and couldn't believe the mess. "You two ought to be ashamed of yourselves for not staying at my house like I asked. You have no idea the kind of danger you put yourselves in. Crazy killers are on the loose and you scared me to death when I got home today and you weren't there."

Elsa started to cry. "I called you several times."

Sylvia came to her defense. "Si, she really did. Six or seven times at least."

"I'm angry," he said.

His mother cried. "I'm sorry. Like I said, I called you but you never answered."

Mario felt terrible. Never again would he refuse a call from his mother, no matter what the circumstances. "Okay. I know. I'm sorry I didn't call you back. God if anything happened to you..."

Elsa brushed her fingers through his wavy hair. "You did your best. We're fine."

"*Si* and you should have stayed put."

"*Si*, I know."

"I'm not happy with you, Mama, but what's done is done. We need to concentrate on Angela. Speaking of that, Benito offered to send a car for us and..." He checked his watch. "...he should be here any minute now. We've got to get changed."

Elsa threw up her hands. "Look at me. I'm a mess. I haven't had time to get ready."

"What are you talking about? You've had plenty of time."

"No, I did what you told me and I stayed right here, just like you said."

"Oh Mama." He put his arms around her, kissed her cheek. "You know I love you. Come on and let's go check out the house and get you ready. I still need to put my suit on."

They walked next door and Mario couldn't help his emotions when he saw his family home torn to shreds. "I can't believe this." He rubbed the knot on his head. "But you two shouldn't have cleaned any of this up. How are the policia going to investigate?"

"What happened to your head?" Elsa asked. "You have a bump."

"Si, I hit it." Mario didn't want to upset his mother by telling her about the shooting this morning. Things were clearly stressful enough.

"You need to have someone look at that." She slid her arm around his waist and her face twisted up when she felt the hard vest underneath his shirt. "What is this?"

"Nothing." He changed the subject and pulled away. "Show me what happened before you cleaned this up."

Elsa wouldn't let up. "It's something, Mario. Tell me what it is."

He sighed. "Nothing."

"Well," Elsa sighed. "If you say so."

"Good, now show me."

 Elsa pointed to the empty hole in the front of her house. "The window was torn out, the phone was off the hook in the kitchen and all the bills and papers were…"

"What? The phone was off the hook? Are you sure?"
"Si."

"Good. I'll have our guys check the phone records then. Go on…"

His mother continued her tour of the place, finally picking up Angela's cracked photo, "And then there is this. I wanted to take it today to the funeral. It is the best picture…" She broke off in tears.

He put his arms around her. "I hate this happened. I hate I wasn't here to protect you, and as much as I love you, I hate you and Sylvia cleaning this up. I must find the people who did this to our family and I will not stop until I do. Here, give me that." He took Angela's photo from the frame, picking the glass from it and throwing it away before slipping it back into the frame, "See? Still beautiful. This will work for today, okay? Now, everything will be alright

once I am finished being mad at you for leaving this morning." He kissed her cheek.

"What was I supposed to do? I couldn't reach you, family's coming today to eat…" She felt around, ran her arm up toward the shoulder, "What is this? It feels like some kind of vest. Aren't you hot?"

Mario backed away, removing her hands. "No, I'm fine. You go on and get changed."

Elsa wouldn't let up. "But aren't you too hot?"

He wished he had two more vests for his mother and Sylvia. "No, now go on. I still need to get changed."

"Oh alright, but I think you should try to wear less clothes in summer. You would feel better."

"Si, mama."

"It's not good for people to get overheated." She disappeared into the back.

Mario shook his head and smiled. "Okay."

Sylvia appeared in the doorway. "Hola. I'm ready now."

"Great. Have a seat here, I guess." He brushed the broken glass and debris off of the old sofa.

"Sorry. We tried to clean that up, I see we missed some." Sylvia sat down and ran her fingers through her long black hair.

"No problemo. We will help you clean up your place later." He never noticed Sylvia before. He only met her a few times. She was a very pretty lady, even when she had been up all night crying. He felt sorry for her, and his mother. And now their homes were destroyed too. Tonight they would stay with him, no matter what. He shut the door. "Wait here, okay? Keep an eye out the window. The car should be here soon."

Mario went in his old room and changed into his suit, despite having to step over the contents of his mother's sewing and mending supplies. Her spare patches of fabric scattered around the floor, along with pins, needles and a few patterns from when he and Angela were little. He started to bend over to pick it all up, his first instinct told him to clean it, but he knew there wasn't any time right now, besides, the relatives and friends would primarily be in the living room today, not in here. He put on his only white dress shirt, carefully buttoning it up to the top, and wrapped his tie around his neck. His pants were slightly too tight, but they looked clean and would work okay. He closed the door behind him and went out to the living room, holding the two ends of his tie in his hands. "Is my mom out yet?"

"No," Sylvia said.

"Oh. Can you help me with this?"

Sylvia stood and walked over to him. "*Si.*" She carefully tied the knot and cinched it tight to his neck. "There you go."

Standing still, watching Sylvia fix his tie, relaxed him more than he cared to admit. He liked the smell of Sylvia's perfume and the way her hair brushed against his wrists.

He should not think of such things. Her son Carlos was only a few years younger than him. "Thank you."

Outside a black car with tinted windows pulled up. Mario's first instinct was to hit the floor and tell everyone in the house to duck or run for their lives, but once it parked, a well appointed driver went around to a side door, two uniformed officers stepped out, and helped Bene out of the car. He walked up the gravel walkway and knocked.

Mario was impressed. Bene not only brought a limo, he came to get the family himself. He couldn't help but wonder how different and exciting their lives might have been if Angela lived and she and Bene married. The possibilities were endless...

He opened the door just as Bene started to knock. "Benito." They shook hands. "Gracias for coming out here."

Bene looked far more somber than this morning when he and Mario laughed themselves silly in the office. He took off his dark sunglasses, combed his hair back with his hand and smiled slightly. "I told you there is no place I would rather be. My father and Rita stayed behind, but they wanted to tell you—"

"It's okay, please come in." Mario nearly laughed when he saw the look on Sylvia's star struck face when Presidente Benito Juarez stepped into their tiny living room. "Oh Bene, this is Sylvia, our next door neighbor."

Bene smiled and offered his hand. "I am so sorry about your son, Mrs. Ortiz. Mario and I will do everything in our power to find the people who did this and I want to personally thank you on behalf of myself and my family. Carlos saved my life, and I am forever grateful."

Sylvia took to instant stammering and could barely form an intelligible word. Finally she managed, "Oh…"

Mario bit his lip to keep from laughing. He noticed the way the women looked at Benito. So much for his own magical moment with Sylvia now that Bene arrived…

And Angela and Benito? They were like magic, pure beauty and charisma. Everyone wanted to be with them, photograph them, read about them in the trashy tabloid magazines, see them on TV or hear about every one of their comings and goings. They were a super stunning couple who were unfortunately never meant to be.

"I'm ready," Elsa announced. All eyes turned to see her. She stood in the doorway to the living room wearing a short sleeved plain black dress with a small hat and veil. She rarely wore makeup, but today she wore eyeliner, mascara and lipstick.

Bene stepped forward. "Mrs. Martinez, I am so sorry about Angela."

Mario held his breath, hoping his mother wouldn't start on any of her rampages.

"Gracias, Benito. Thank you for coming." Elsa looked at the ground and her tears already started to smear her makeup. She dabbed her eyes with a Kleenex. "I know my Angela would have wanted you with us today."

Mario sighed relief. "Ready to go, Mama?" He noticed Elsa wore the only black dress she had to her name, the same one she wore when his father died years ago. He just now remembered his father died in the heat of summer too, only in August.

He put his arm around Elsa, careful to guide her to the door this time so she couldn't feel his vest he still chose to wear under his suit today. Mario wasn't too sure if any of them would be safe out in the open of the cemetery, but he didn't want to take any chances. He needed the confidence to throw himself in front of a bullet to save his family, if necessary, and although his new vest was uncomfortable, it gave him that feeling of security. Plus Benito would surely have secret service with him. Mario hoped it would be enough.

Elsa gazed out the front door and saw the car. She brought her hands to her mouth. "A limo? Oh God how I wish this wasn't my only chance to ride in a limo."

The other day, Mario offhandedly mentioned to Bene about his mother's lifelong dream of riding in a limo. Logistically speaking, the car made sense size wise for so many people, and once Bene heard about it, he apparently made sure to get one. He listened and obviously cared. Mario respected him for that.

"Mrs. Martinez, I promise I will see to it personally this will not be your only limo ride, okay?" Bene smiled and held Elsa's hand as they all climbed into the car to head for the funeral service.

Thirty Seven

After receiving his phone call this morning, Dennis Montoya locked himself in the quiet solitude of his home office for the entire rest of the day. He needed to study up on the Aztec customs and rituals in order to adequately prepare for tonight and effectively lead his people through this time of transition.

He thought about the disastrous events of July 1st and smiled. One man's mess proved to be his opportunity.

The Montoya household always seemed quiet during the weekdays. His wife worked as a secretary in a doctor's office and his sons were grown and away at college, a perfect situation for private reflection.

Dennis still couldn't believe the meeting place for tonight, *Cerro de la Estrella*, or Hill of the Star. Regardless of what his superior thought, Montoya initially felt this location was far too public for such sacred endeavors.

He changed his mind after researching the site. In times of old, Cerro de la Estrella served as the location for the Aztec ancestors New Fire Temple. Aztec priests observed the heavens from this temple every fifty two years and determine whether or not the gods would destroy the world or allow it to continue another fifty two years.

Since *Noche Triste* just passed and the stars aligned during their botched attempt to rid the world of *Quetzalcoatl*, tonight would determine the course of their future destiny and reveal whether the gods were pleased or angered by recent events.

Despite his excitement about his recent promotion, Montoya had a horrible feeling about tonight he couldn't explain. He went over in his head, and no matter how many times he imagined the ceremonies, the ominous feeling lingered, although he could not put his finger on why. Montoya felt honored to be chosen to preside over El Templo, but the means by which he rose to power still felt questionable.

If his predecessor properly carried out the sacrifice of *Quetzalcoatl* in accordance to plan, things would be different. Hard headed Pena changed locations last minute without telling anyone, and disrupted a Catholic festival in the process. His foolishness put everyone in the entire El Templo organization at risk. Between Judge Pena's irresponsibility and the meddling Martinez, Montoya couldn't help but worry the identity of their entire group was jeopardized and something would inevitably go wrong.

Montoya poured through his books on Aztec ritual, researched various points on the internet. All the particulars about the rituals flooded back to his memory. Tonight they would meet, set future plans, look at the stars, and prepare for the ritual through cleansing. *Everything would be okay*, he told himself.

If all went well, they would perform a necessary sacrifice to further appease the gods, and light a new fire to be carried to every member's home in the modern Aztec Empire known as El Templo.

Montoya wondered what ever happened to Father Salazar and if he would be the chosen sacrifice for tonight's ritual. He assumed so.

Supposedly the group took Salazar to a secure location after Martinez searched the tunnels the other day, and tonight he would offer the aging priest to the hungry gods. Montoya shivered thinking about it. He'd never been granted permission to perform the sacrifice himself before. He hoped he could do it. He witnessed many such rituals during his fifteen plus years in the organization, but normally these consisted of the homeless or people who wouldn't be missed. To think tonight he would sacrifice such a high profile figure seemed both exciting and ominous.

Before the ceremony, he would need a bit more information about the specific plans and sacrificial methods so he could wisely lead his people into their new life.

***

The man in black leather didn't have much time. He pulled his jacket off, stuffed it into a shopping bag he carried into the hospital this afternoon, and quickly donned the plain blue scrubs and surgical facemask of hospital life. He ran his fingers through his hair to mess it up a bit before pulling out his reading glasses and putting them on. Now he would fit in here.

He noticed Salazar's clothes folded neatly in a corner and stuffed them into the bag, hanging it on the wheelchair in the corner of the room. Today John Doe # 3 would be mysteriously discharged from care.

He lifted Father Salazar into the wheelchair, carefully leaned his head back on a head rest so as to make him simply look sleepy, and opened the door to his room.

The man formerly in black leather couldn't believe how easily he pulled off these crimes by blending in and remembering to avoid eye contact. He always chuckled to himself after a job, and today, he might go so far as to propose a toast to himself. This job truly took the cake, and if he had his way, this would only be the first of many exciting events today.

He wheeled Salazar down the hall of the cardiac ward, loaded him carefully on the elevator, and wheeled him outside to the passenger pickup area of the hospital. He put the emergency brakes on the wheelchair and dashed around the corner, ditched his uniform in his backseat and pulled around to the pickup area like any concerned relative would. He loaded his patient into his car, and sped away before anyone realized what happened.

Thirty Eight

"Ashes to ashes, dust to dust…" The funeral for Angela Martinez was a graceful yet somber event.

After a quiet and beautiful Mass, family and friends stood around the gravesite as each of them put a handful of dirt on Angela's coffin and said their goodbyes.

The words of the priest sounded like a distant hum to Mario, who could hardly believe this was happening. His sister should still be alive. She had so many gifts, so much life yet to live, and yet, here she was in a box in the plot next to his father which was reserved for his mother, not Angela.

The explosion of events over the past few days proved so painful and shocking, Mario pushed Angela as far from his mind as he could until this moment. Now he stared into the grave and faced the terrible fact he would never see his older sister ever again. The life they all would have had together, the things they would have done, all the hopes, dreams, fears were all gone. He felt too stunned to cry any more tears for her, at least not now, not here. He glanced at his mother.

Elsa's tears were enough for them all today. She refused to throw dirt on her daughter's coffin, repeatedly sobbing and crying about how grateful she was their father hadn't lived to see this day. Mario agreed. His father couldn't survive this.

Benito stood tall, his hands clasped in front of him, his bloodshot eyes covered, like Mario's, with dark sunglasses.

From a hedge in a far corner of the cemetery, Mario heard the sound of flashbulbs and saw the bright lights from the corners of his eyes as the paparazzi stole photos of Bene in his darkest hour. Why did they insist on hounding his family? Angela never asked for that kind of fame.

Benito couldn't help it either. Transparency seemed a necessary evil of his position.

Mario took a deep breath and forced himself to calm down and try and ignore them, even though he thought about running over there and destroying their cameras by tossing them to the ground and stomping on them. Maybe then the media would know how he felt about not having a sister anymore. Perhaps they would understand his feelings about having his entire life destroyed a few days ago. He thought about Bella and her utterly self-absorbed and selfish attitude and knew there would be no way any of these people would think twice about his feelings. They only wanted the scoop and the big break.

He thought again about the satisfaction he would get by crushing them, but in the same moment, realized he couldn't. It would not be right or fair to anyone and would only cause his mother more pain. He must be strong, but he made a silent vow right there and then as he looked into the ground that no matter what, he would put a stop to the people who ended his sister's life. This investigation proved the organization was far more complex than anyone ever imagined, but none of that mattered. He would stop at nothing to put an end to these people, even if it cost him his life in the process.

He also knew to be careful for his mother's sake. She was his sole responsibility now.

Mario came back from the faraway place when he noticed the priest stopped talking. Everyone else took a few steps back as the men finished pouring the dirt on to the grave. Mario felt numbness in his hands and arms. He accidentally dropped the memorial write up on Angela on the ground and bent over to retrieve it. He studied her picture. There she was, forever young and beautiful.

His mother's tears finally ended, for now at least. Sylvia put her arm around Elsa and her sisters gathered tightly around her as they slowly began to leave.

Benito stayed the longest. He appeared immune to the flashbulbs and cameras right now.

Mario walked up to him. "Bene?"

"I can't believe she's gone." A tear streamed down his face and he clutched Mario's shoulder.

Mario remembered what he brought in his jacket pocket and knew this would be the right thing to do. He pulled out the gold heart necklace and handed it to him. "Here."

Bene took it, lowered his sunglasses slightly to have a closer look. "What is this?"

Mario gulped. "A necklace I gave Angela when we were kids. We used to be best friends growing up. I'm not sure we still were since I'd been away the last year or two, but she wore this always as a promise to me of our love for each other. I think she would want you to have it. She was wearing it the day she died."

Benito clutched the necklace in his fist and fought back tears. On the back side of the heart, the inscription read: *I love you Mi Hermana.* "Are you sure?"

Mario nodded.

Bene swallowed hard trying to keep composure. "Thank you. I'll treasure this forever."

Bene reached inside his suit pocket, pulled out a small box and handed it to Mario. "Here."

Mario noticed the paparazzi hid in the bushes snapping pictures of their tears. He clenched his jaw. "What's this?"

"Open it."

He pulled the lid off and pulled out the velvet box inside, opened it up and gasped at the beautiful solitaire diamond ring. "Wow."

Bene sniffled. "I was going to give this to her this weekend. I had it all planned out, a trip to Puerto Vallarta, the beach, some champagne, but now…" Tears fell down his cheeks. "I should've done it sooner. I wish she knew how I felt and what I wanted."

"I know she did." Mario handed it back. "Here."

Bene shook his head. "No, you keep it. I thought about putting it on her finger so she could wear it into eternity, but since I never got a chance to ask her, I didn't think that would be appropriate, and thought it might upset your mother. Besides, that would be a waste. I hope you will save it and someday, when you meet someone special, you can give it to her."

Mario held it in his hand, wishing Angela were here. "I don't know. You should give it—"

Benito pushed it away. "I would never give that to anyone but Angela."

Mario respected that. "But this must cost—"

"I don't care about the money. God I wish I gave this to her. I wanted to marry her more than anything in the whole world, and now it's all gone. Please take it. Do it as a favor to me. I can't bear to keep it and I believe Angela would want you to have it, just as she would want me to have this. We will exchange these and call it even."

Mario shrugged and put it in his pocket. "Okay. Thank you."

"No, thank you." He rubbed the necklace in his fingers. "I treasure this."

The two men stood and watched as the workers patted down the final bit of dirt with their shovels, got into their utility truck and slowly drove away. Bene and Mario stared at the freshly upturned earth and shared a moment of silence together before each of them dropped a rose atop the gravesite and walked off to join the rest of the family.

Thirty Nine

Once the media cleared from the murder in the Zocalo, Bella and Pedro responded to a call she received earlier from the Juarez Hospital Security Department. After the way they treated her the last time she came here, she didn't want to go at all, but the man on the phone sounded urgent.

She walked into the lobby, relieved to see a new woman behind the counter. "Bella Perez. I'm here to see the…"

"Yes, Miss Perez. We've been waiting for you." The woman picked up the phone and rang someone, "Have a seat."

"Come on, Pedro." They sat in the stuffy crowded waiting room. Bella liked the way the woman recognized her on sight. Fame had those kind of advantages...

Within a minute, a man in a plain dress shirt and slacks walked up. "Miss Perez? I'm the supervisor here. Thank you for coming."

She smiled and extended her hand, half expecting him to kiss her fingers, which he didn't. "Hello, thank you for calling." She and Pedro followed him into the back where a heavy set kid sat with his feet on a table while he watched ten security screens at once.

"Jose." the supervisor said, "Get your feet off that table. We've got company."

Jose's eyes got wide when he saw Bella, a reaction she was more than used to by now. "*Hola.*"

"Miss Perez," the supervisor said. "Occasionally we get people admitted into the hospital anonymously and today, while reviewing some tapes, we found something newsworthy."

Her heart always raced a little at words like that. "Oh?"

"Go on, Jose, play it," the supervisor said.

Jose pushed a button or two and Bella watched as a tall kid with a black hooded shirt and jeans dropped a man in the lobby of the hospital, shouted out and ran.

Normally Bella didn't think much about such calls. She worked as a reporter for so long, most days one story blended into the next, but when she saw the man on the screen, her hand went to her mouth. "I need the tape."

"You've got it," the supervisor said.
***

When Bella and Pedro got outside, she was furious her boss insisted she and Pedro grab the van and race up to the northern poor section of Mexico City rather than running the story about the video right away. She argued with her boss, but as always, it didn't matter. He wanted what he wanted.

Nearly an hour later, she and Pedro finally reached their exit. Bella hated this neighborhood. Everyone knew nothing ever went on out there and shootings were almost a daily occurrence with too much frequency to be considered anything newsworthy.

They parked the van at the end of a huge line of TV trucks at the bottom of the hill. She resented the money it cost to repair her heels and she would ask her boss for reimbursement.

"What is this?" Pedro asked her.

"I don't know," she flipped her hair back, twisting it in a knot so the sweat from the summer heat wouldn't make it droop. "I told them we need to stay downtown where all the action is."

"Must be something..." Pedro said.

"Whatever. Hurry up and let's get this over with."

As they climbed the top of the hill, Bella noticed the number of media outlets spying on the funeral of some apparent nobody and wondered what in the world could possibly be so interesting to warrant CNN and the major players to be here. "Keep the camera off until I say so, Pedro. I don't think..."

Bella gestured him to stop and she pushed her way through the paparazzi up to the thick row of trees on the east side of the property. She saw a large family gathered in black, but nothing special, until she got just a little closer, and finally it hit her. Mario Martinez stood next to *Presidente Benito Juarez*. Now it all made sense. She knew why he had been such a jerk.

Pedro walked over. "Well? Should I roll?"

Bella shook her head. "No. There's nothing here. Let's go."

Forty

S ister Lucia Hernandez and the rest of the nuns at Cathedral Metropolitano prayed continuously for the safe return of their leader, Archbishop Father Salazar, and for their own release from the stone prison where they were held ever since the other night.

The Sister thought often about the night when Mario Martinez came and asked her about the whereabouts of the nuns. She tried to tell him with her eyes to look behind her at the man who held the gun to her back, but he didn't seem to notice. She thought about the young choir boy and how she begged her captor to allow him to leave unharmed. Still, nobody questioned the strange silence in the Cathedral and when she made up the story about the nunnery down the road, she hoped Martinez recognized her lie and seen the fear in her eyes that night, but perhaps he didn't know all the nuns resided in their church. She replayed her poor choice of words in her mind a thousand times these past few days, wondering if she said it differently or done something else, if she and the other nuns would be free right now. No, she told herself. This situation played out in accordance to God's plan, and although she didn't understand the meaning and lessons she should glean from this torture at the present time, there was a reason. All would be revealed in time.

Now she and all her fellow Sisters were detained in the cold caverns beneath the church. Some of the older women complained about their joints and bones aching in the cold, while the younger girls shivered and cried. She tried to speak softly to them, tell them to relax and to never show their fear to the people who held them.

The captors checked on them and fed them regularly. Whenever they showed up, the sisters said nothing to them and kept all emotion to themselves. Sister Hernandez told the group to keep faith and spend these confined hours in prayer, because only in the prayerful state could they be at peace with the situation.

Sister Hernandez didn't hear a word regarding Father Salazar as of yet. She hoped the captors might say something she could overhear, but so far, nothing. Deep in her soul, she felt her mentor was still alive. A soul as grand as his would surely be felt leaving, and so far, she felt nothing in regards to Salazar. She prayed God would produce a miracle for everyone concerned, because in her humble opinion, only a miracle would save any of them now.

She knew what happened with Benito Juarez and how, despite lost hope, he eventually returned safely. She prayed God still had use for them and would not call them into His heavenly presence yet. She still had much to do yet on earth in helping her people, teaching them the ways of Catholicism.

As for Father Salazar, he did so much good for so many, Sister Hernandez truly believed his work still needed to touch many more lives in their city.

The Sister quietly contemplated the current crime rate in these times. With new organized crime operations like these, Sister Hernandez felt the people of Mexico City needed their church more than ever before.

She fell to her knees, prayed she would find strength to continue leading her fellow sisters another day through this trying time, and realized if God called them home, she must freely let go into the hereafter.

Sister heard the sounds of footsteps coming down the stairs. A tall man in a black leather jacket with grey streaked hair and a sinister face stood in the doorway. "You're all still on your knees, are you?" he laughed. "There's no amount of prayer to save any of you. You're all going to die soon, right alongside your beloved Father Salazar." He threw several loaves of bread down on the floor. "Eat up, sisters. This meal will be your last."

Some of the nuns broke their vows of silence and cried at the man's evil proclamation. Sister Hernandez prayed they hold their tongues just a little longer while they listened to the sounds of the man's footsteps going up the stairs and the sound of the lock on the door as he closed them in once more for who knew how long.

"What are we going to do?" one of the younger nuns cried. "We're all going to die."

"They've probably already killed Father Salazar," cried another.

"Hush," Sister Hernandez said. "I told you all to quiet your fears and be strong. God has a plan. I believe someone will find us once they notice we are not in the Sanctuary. We must keep faith."

"Yes, but what about Father Salazar?" one of them cried. "The man said he is dead."

Sister Hernandez shook her head. "No, I have faith Father Salazar is still alive and well and he will be returned to us."

"But what if he isn't? What if they kill us all?" another cried.

"Hush up and resume your silent vows. You should all be ashamed of yourselves for thinking otherwise. Have faith. Bow your heads in prayer and let us keep our hope. God will find a way. I know it."

Forty One

Rita spent a quiet afternoon in the Palacio while Benito attended Angela's funeral and Stefano Juarez attended to personal business outside the office.

Since she began her new position as Presidential Secretary, quiet afternoons like this were becoming increasingly rare, and she relished the time to be one with her thoughts.

She kept a small television set in her office for days like today. Sometimes she enjoyed listening to one of the soap operas in the background while she did her filing. Today, something told her to turn it on.

"…I'm Bella Perez reporting. This just in, we have new video footage of the Good Samaritan who arrived at the hospital late yesterday afternoon."

Rita put her hands on her heart. She always loved hearing stories about selflessly people helping one another.

"…but take a look at this. When our news team did a close up, does this man look like anyone you know?"

The blown up image on the screen was placed next to a photo of the missing Father Salazar.

"Si, we believe this is Father Salazar, who has reportedly been missing since the evening of July 1st. Also just in, the Samaritan's ID was just confirmed by Mexico City police as this man…"

As the screen flashed to the shooting victim killed the day before, Rita held her hands to her mouth.

"Si, this young man, shot to death on the steps of Cathedral Metropolitano only yesterday is none other than Tony Guzman, eldest son of Antonio Guzman who was found dead in *Plaza de la Constitucion* earlier this afternoon. Random coincidence?" Bella asked her audience. "I don't think so."

Rita's hand trembled. She turned off the television and scribbled the information on a notepad. She hated to call Benito this afternoon, but with news like this, she knew she had to interrupt. She picked up the phone, hardly able to believe this incredible turn of events. Maybe things would be okay after all, she thought, and dialed Bene's private number.

   ***

Bene politely stayed at Mrs. Martinez' home and ate a bowl of her *menudo* and homemade *tamales* and *tortillas* after the funeral services. He talked to her sisters and the rest of the family and listened to everyone reminisce and tell stories about the woman he loved and lost when something crunched under the heel of his shoe. He bent down, surprised to see a shard of glass. "Oh no, I hope I didn't break something," he told Mario.

Mario got a strange look on his face. "No, you didn't do that."

"What's wrong?"

Mario pulled Bene aside and whispered in his ear. "I didn't want to mention it before, but someone broke in here sometime between last night and this morning."

"What? Why didn't you tell me? We need to get a security detail out here to stay the night."

"Si, they broke into Sylvia's house next door too."

Bene got a knot in his stomach. He scowled and looked around the house. "This happened when?"

"Earlier today. My mom and her cleaned up the best they could, but I don't have a good feeling about it. I think I need to move them tonight, don't you?"

Bene's mind raced a mile a minute. "*Si*. I'm considering putting the entire family and Sylvia up in a hotel with some guard service for a few days until this mess blows over. What do you think they would say to that?"

"I think you know by now, my mom is stubborn, but yes, I think it's a good idea. They could always come to my house, though."

"You decide Mario, but I don't mind the expense. Think about it." Bene heard his phone ringing in his jacket pocket. In the old days before he was Presidente, he would never leave a phone on at an event like this, but now, he had no choice. He pulled it out, glanced at it and saw it was Rita. "Will you excuse me?" Bene cupped the receiver with his palm. "Rita, the funeral is over now, but I'm at the Martinez' house and I can't talk—"

"Bene." Rita sounded upset. "Is Mario still with you?"

"Si, he's right here, why? What's wrong?"

"I just saw Father Salazar on TV. He's at a hospital near downtown."

Bene could hardly believe his ears. "What a break. Hang on, let me grab Mario. He needs to get over there right away."

"*Si*. I will call the hospital myself in a minute."

Bene ran the options through in his mind. "No Rita, you better wait. I don't want anyone getting wind of this, in case it jeopardizes Father Salazar's safety."

"But *Senor*, the photos are already all over the television. The Guzman boy dropped him off over there yesterday."

"Guzman? You mean the kid who…"

"*Si*."

Bene's head started to spin. "I have a bad feeling about this Rita. Mario and I both better come downtown right away."

"*Si, senor*, please hurry."

"We will be there as soon as we can, Rita, and meanwhile, you keep the television on and call me with any new updates. We shouldn't be more than an hour."

"An *hour*? Please do better than that. Hurry."

Bene realized Rita was right. They might not have much time. "I'll grab Mario and we'll leave now, okay? *Adios and gracias.*" Bene hung up and walked through the crowded living room. He found Mario stuffing a pastry in his mouth while talking to an old lady in a wheelchair.

One of Mario's aunts batted her eyes at Bene and started heading right toward him. "*Senor Presidente…*"

"Excuse me," he told her. "I need a word with Mario. I'll be right back…"Bene gave a nod to his secret service patrol, who walked into the street to clear the way for them to leave. "Hey Mario."

Mouth full, Mario turned around and the unspoken bond between them said something was wrong without Bene saying another word. "*Now?*"

"Si," Bene said. "I need to find your mother and say goodbye."

Mario reached his arm above the shorter primarily female crowd and pointed to Elsa who was busy cooking something in the kitchen.

Benito went to the kitchen, kissed Elsa's cheek, thanked her, and met Mario at the door. "Let's go. Now."

"What's up?" Mario asked.

"Get in the car and I'll tell you. You're not going to believe it."

Forty Two

Mario stood in his mother's front yard, about to step into the car when he heard a familiar voice call him.

"Wait." Elsa threw her apron aside and ran after him.

He promised himself he would never ignore her again, so he turned around and met her on the porch. "Mama. Bene and I have a lead. I will call you in a couple hours, okay?" He kissed her cheek.

"Be careful you two," Elsa smiled and waved at Bene. Mario knew then and there Benito successfully worked his magic on her, just like he did with everyone he met. Thank God for that. Bene was a permanent fixture in their lives as far as Mario was concerned.

Bene tapped his watch. "*Now*."

"Mama, I love you, I hate we need to leave, but it's urgent. You'll be safe here with the security people, okay?" He held Elsa's hands.

"Okay, okay. Go on and call me, will you?"

"I promise." He climbed into the waiting car.

On the way back to the city center, Bene told Mario all about the phone call. "What? You mean Salazar has been right under our noses this whole time?"

"Can you believe it?" Bene said. "What's even more troubling is who took him in yesterday."

"Who?"

"Tony Guzman."

"No."

"*Si.*"

"Well I've got news for you too. Guzman Senior is dead, gunned down in the Zocalo this afternoon. Also, I got this…from Amelia Sanchez." Mario removed the business card from his pocket and handed it to Bene.

"Guzman's business card?" he said. "What about it?"

"Turn it over. Senora Sanchez says she found this in Dennis Montoya's things today. This is an Aztec Symbol for Death and War."

Bene studied the card. "What could all of this possibly mean? Is Montoya involved?"

"It wouldn't surprise me. He gave me a terrible time about searching that tunnel the other day and in the end, he had the keys to it all along. I can't help but wonder if Montoya tipped them off and knew about Salazar's whereabouts all along." Mario ran a hand through his hair, "Agh. And to think poor Salazar has been round here all along. This is all my fault. I should have worked the leads better."

"No. How could you know? Besides, with all the shootings and Angela's funeral... It looks like everything is going to turn out alright anyhow. Go pick up Salazar, and we can get everything back to normal."

Mario raised his eyebrows. "You think?"

Benito lowered his eyes. "No. Things will never be the same for me ever again."

Mario agreed. Life as they knew it ended for good. Even if they found the people responsible. "So did you find out why Salazar was in the hospital?"

"Heart attack from what Rita heard on TV."

"Really?"

Bene nodded. " He had open heart surgery yesterday."

Mario put his hand on his spinning head to try and wrap his mind around everything. "Unbelievable. Why would the younger Guzman take Father Salazar to the hospital if the group planned to kill him all along?"

Bene scratched his head. "I don't know. Do you think Salazar intimidated him?"

"Intimidated Tony Guzman? The kid was a mammoth."

"I don't know…"

"Because he's a man of the cloth. I know my priest always made me feel a little nervous."

Bene shrugged. "It would be difficult to accost a priest, don't you think? I couldn't do it."

Mario laughed. "That's good to know!"

Bene rolled his eyes and smiled for the first time all afternoon.

"Maybe that gesture of human kindness is why he and his old man are dead today. My guess is the surgery messed up their plans, big time."

"Maybe," Bene said.

"Both Guzman's were most likely involved in your kidnapping as well as all the murders," Mario said.

"Probably. But now they're dead, so who killed them?"

Mario wished he knew. "*Yo no se.*"

"Did you hear from the team at Santa Cecilia yet?"

"No. I wanted to get over there today but by the time Guzman got gunned down, and Amelia Sanchez called me over and my mom's place got ransacked, I didn't get a chance, why?"

"I'm anxious to find out if they picked up any DNA we can use to identify anyone, that's all."

Mario laughed. "Believe me, there's so much blood in the interior temple there, they'll surely come out with something we can use."

"I hope so. We need to get this contained fast."

"Why? So your people won't think you're a liar for telling them the city is safe?"

Bene sighed. "The media must be having a field day with this after all these shootings. I want to make our city safe again."

"You will. I have faith."

Bene nodded. "I appreciate that, but it's you, Mario, who does most of the work so far. If we are successful, it will be you the citizens should thank."

Mario sighed. "That's what's so frustrating about the whole situation. If people like the Guzman's and the District Court Judge Pena are involved, there's no telling how deep this thing goes."

"I know…"

"We need more help, Bene. I've got some ideas, but first we need to get Salazar back home safe."

They rode in silence for the next several minutes. Mario stared out the window at the mountains and watched the long lines of cars on the expressway. He thought about everything that happened so far with the case, from finding the passage under the church, to Carlos' death, the many shootings. He hoped to find Salazar alive and well and ready to talk once he arrived at the hospital. Maybe he could finally find the people responsible for all this and put an end to the violence once and for all. "You mentioned Rita saw this all on television, right?"

Bene continued looking out the window. "*Si.*"

Suddenly Mario remembered someone who might be able to help him.

Forty Three

Bella paced around the top floor office and watched the fluffy clouds outside, while trying her best to let her boss' rampage go in one ear, out the next.

"What? You mean you didn't get any footage of El Presidente at his girlfriend's funeral? How could you be so *stupido?*"

Bella hated when her boss screamed at her. He'd been fairly lenient lately, thanks to some of her right-place-right-time luck, but today, he was mad as a hornet. "I am a journalist with professional integrity," she said. "You should have seen him. He looked so sad. It wasn't worth exploiting another human being like that."

"What are you talking about, Bella? Please don't tell me you've gone soft on me now, right when we're getting ready to get a reputation for breaking news. I need you out there tailing Juarez for anything and everything you can get on him from here on out, comprende?"

"Besides…" She pushed past his desk and pressed her hands on his spotless window. "I broke the stories about the Guzman's, or did you forget CNN requested our feed today?"

"I don't care what you did when, Bella. When I give you an assignment, I expect you to do it."

Bella was saved by her ringing cell and the caller ID. Mario Martinez. "Well I have an inside scoop to the real story right here," she shouted, holding up her cell so the boss could see the name. "El Presidente's best friend, Mario Martinez. He talks to me and only me, and I plan to get the real story, the private interview with El Presidente and I will succeed in doing it by not taking the cheap shots like everyone else in town."

Her boss immediately softened up, "Oh, okay, wonderful. Let me know what he says."

The phone stopped ringing before she could answer. "I have to go call him back. Mario Martinez doesn't like to be kept waiting, so if you'll excuse me…" She clicked back to her cubicle in the far corner of the newsroom, daydreaming about getting one of the corner offices once she got this story. She redialed and he answered, first ring. "Mario. Bella. *Que pasa*? What's up?"

"I heard you covered a story about a Good Samaritan who helped Father Salazar in the hospital last night and that person happened to be your ex, Tony Guzman, correct?"

"*Si.*"

"Who did you talk to about it? Who told you?"

Bella giggled and twisted her hair around her finger. "Mr. Martinez, I don't divulge my sources…"

"Please, Bella. I need to get to Salazar immediately. He's in grave danger. Did you see him or not?"

"No."

"How did you find out about the Samaritan video?"

"I told you, Mr. Martinez, I do not divulge sources."

"Bella, this is a police matter, whether you realize it or not. You tell me right now, or…"

"Or what?"

"Or Benito will grant me a warrant for your arrest."

She laughed. "You can't do that."

"Want to try me? Benito is sitting here now. I won't hesitate to have his secretary type something up for me."

She sighed. "I don't know…"

"What? Are you afraid I'll tell CNN?"

She thought about it. "You might…"

"I won't. I need to get Father Salazar back and I need to find out if anyone out there saw him in that hospital today so please tell me who gave you access to that video? Please."

Bella filed a chipped edge from her nail. "The security people at Juarez Hospital. There. Are you happy now? Not such a big top secret, is it?"

"Thank you. Did they happen to say they saw Salazar?"

"No. They didn't say a word about him."

"Thank you. Next time you get a lead like this, will you promise to bring it to me first before you air it?"

"I don't know, depends on what kinds of leads you're willing to give me," she said as she reviewed her manicure under the fluorescent lights of her office.

"Name your price. What do you want?"

"Seriously?"

"Yep."

"I want an exclusive private interview with Benito Juarez."

"To discuss what?"

"The nature of his relationship with your sister."

"You know, Bella, you really are a sleaze. I suppose you hid in the bushes this afternoon along with the rest of the sharks, didn't you?"

"Actually…"

"Never mind. I don't want to know."

"Yes, I was there, but if you'll notice, I was the only reporter who chose not to film the two of you in your private moment by her grave."

"Oh really? And I suppose you want a medal of honor for that?"

"You know what I want."

"Yes and you're not going to get it."

"Well then I guess you're not going to get inside information about my stories then."

She heard Mario sigh. "Okay. Let me work on it."

"Can you pull that off?"

"Probably, but for now I need you to tell me everything you know about this case. Since we're dealing with a kidnapping, I remind you withholding evidence is a crime."

She sighed. "I already told you what I know, and I promise I will come to you about anything else I find out, but you better help me get my big break."

"I will help you, but there's something still bothering me. Please, Bella. There are evil men who want Salazar dead for some reason. Please tell me how you got the video. Did you see Salazar? If you did, I promise you won't be in trouble."

"No. I told you. I got a call from the security director of the hospital and he took me there and we watched it. End of story. Honestly I didn't think a thing about Salazar. I was too distracted. When I saw Tony Guzman dead on the steps the other night, I freaked and didn't follow up at all. Please don't tell my boss. He would be furious if he thought I had a chance at a story that big and didn't even think to cover it."

"So you swear that report you gave on TV was basically a bunch of lies?"

"Not lies…"

"But you never saw Salazar."

"No, but…"

"But you implied it on TV, right?"

"Don't you judge me. I have a job to do which involves ratings. I never saw Salazar, but it doesn't take a scientist to see the man in the camera looks just like him."

"As an investigator, didn't you think to go check it out and find the missing man?"

"I told you." Bella shouted. "I freaked out about Tony, okay?"

Several of her coworkers peeked up from their cubicles and walked over to see the commotion.

"You better not be hiding anything, Bella. You're walking a thin line between journalism and jail."

"I did not do anything wrong except for not following up on a lead, okay? I told you what you want to know, now leave me alone, and until you get me that exclusive I will not answer anymore of your questions. Goodbye." she slammed the phone down.

Bella's face felt hot after she got off the phone with Mario. That man was impossible. She looked up and saw her coworkers staring at her, their mouths gaping open. One of them began to clap, and soon, the others joined in a much appreciated round of applause.

"Way to stand up to whoever you were talking to there," a coworker shouted.

Bella hadn't felt that good about herself in months.

Forty Four

Mario hung up the phone after speaking with Bella. God that woman frustrated him.

"Well?" Bene said. "Sounds like you gave someone a hard time."

"I tried Bella Perez, the ditz reporter. She somehow gained access to the video of Tony Guzman at the hospital with Salazar, but says she didn't see him."

"And you believe her?"

"Yes, she's a mess, but I don't think she's a liar. I get so frustrated, though. To be that close to Salazar and lose him now is...Agh!"

"You're too hard on yourself Mario. You found me, I know you'll find the Father too."

The car pulled up in front of the Juarez Hospital where Bene stayed the other night. Mario kicked himself for not checking there. "I still can't believe Salazar's been here this whole time."

Benito patted his shoulder. "You didn't know. It was a fluke. Just go get him and bring him back. I'll be in the office. Call and let me know what you find out."

Mario watched the car pull away. He walked to the main entrance, glanced up at the building, held his breath. Hoping for the best, he ventured inside. With any kind of luck, he would find Salazar alive and well and put an end to all of this mess.

A middle aged woman sat behind a circular desk. Mario handed her a photo of Salazar taken from a church bulletin. "Have you seen him?"

"No, but you're the third person who wanted to know."

"Oh? Who else asked about him?"

She wrinkled her nose. "Why?"

"Did you see the *Presidente's* press conference yesterday?"

"Oh. You're that man from the…"

"*Si.*"

"Oh okay, well, a woman, the TV reporter came by this afternoon to see our supervisor."

"Anyone else?"

"*Si,* another man, older than you, grey streaks here," she pointed to her own temple. "…and here. Nice man. A little overdressed for this time of year…He said that was his father."

"What was he wearing?"

"Black leather jacket, long pants…"

Mario had a bad feeling. "And you gave him the room number?"

"Sure. I was relieved the poor man finally found his family. He had open heart surgery just yesterday but nobody around here knew his name."

"What room is he in? I need to ask him some questions for *El Presidente.*"

The woman gave Mario the number and he ran for the elevators. Once he reached the cardiac ward, he raced down the hall to the room and pushed open the door.

All that remained of Salazar was the empty bed, crumpled sheets, tubes and machines set up for someone who was long gone. "No." Mario stomped his feet. His worst nightmares were now coming to fruition. They obviously got to Father Salazar before he could, thanks to none other than the irresponsible reporting of Bella Perez.

Mario gripped his skull in frustration, turning a circle wondering where to look and what to do next. He found the chart at the foot of the bed, picked it up and read: *John Doe #3 Open heart surgery, stable*

Was this actually Salazar? Mario could only assume. He checked around the room, but it appeared as though even John Doe #3's clothes vanished. Maybe the woman at the desk gave him the wrong John Doe number. If there were three John Doe's, that meant there were at least two others, so he needed to check those people out as well.

Just as he started to go, Mario stepped on something. He bent over to have a closer look. A small crucifix with a medallion of Our Lady of Antigua, namesake of one of the Cathedral's smaller chapels, dangled off of a cross and some pale green glass beads. These might have belonged to Salazar, or they might belong to any faithful person undergoing a major surgery. To make sure, he ran to the nurse's station to tell them what happened. "The man in that room is gone."

Two nurses followed him to the room. "He shouldn't be out of the hospital yet. He had major surgery only yesterday."

"Is this him?" Mario held out the photo.

"Si," they both agreed.

"When was the last time you saw him?"

They looked at each other. "Less than two hours ago, wouldn't you say?" one said to the other.

"Si, I checked him around 1:30 today."

"And both of you worked all afternoon?"

They nodded.

"And neither of you saw him leave?"

"No, we're sorry. We're so overloaded here."

Mario gritted his teeth and held his breath. Father Salazar was here only hours earlier. Now he had to figure out who stole him from his recovery room and where they took him before the aging priest ran out of time.

***

When Bene got back to his office, Rita had the television on. Together they watched the report rerunning on television. "I can't believe it," Bene told her.

"I know. I hope Mario finds him."

"He will," Bene said. "I have a good feeling about it."

The telephone rang and Rita answered. "It's Mario.

Benito hoped he had good news."Did you find him?"

"He's gone. I'm on my way to the church now to see what I can find. Someone took him right out from under their noses sometime this afternoon."

"Keep looking. Let us know." Bene hung up the phone, barely able to hide his disappointment. "He's gone, Rita. We were too late."

"I still believe if anyone can bring Father Salazar back safely, it's Mario."

Bene sighed. "I hope you're right."

Forty Five

Montoya finished his studies and gathered all the items he needed for the ceremony this evening. He dressed in all black and kept his hood tucked away amongst the other items in a box in the trunk of his car.

He took one last look around his office, making sure he hadn't forgotten anything and reached for the handle of his front door, when his wife burst in and surprised him. He jumped and let out a yell.

"Hola dear," she kissed him. "I got off work early and I thought we might get some dinner together."

"I can't."

"Why not, sweetheart?" she reached out for his face.

He slapped her hand away, "Not now. I have things to do." He started pushing past her and walking toward the front door.

"Where are you going?"

Without making any eye contact, he said, "I've got a meeting tonight and I can't be late."

She rolled her eyes. "Oh, with your *group* again? You think those people are more important than your family, Dennis, but you're wrong. You need to stay home with us and stop…"

"Listen here, you. Nothing is more important than my group and the sooner you realize it the better. Goodbye."

***

Mrs. Montoya did not shed a single tear for her wayward husband. She was over it. She realized long ago Dennis was having an extramarital affair, but never could figure out with who. He thought she was stupid and used this idea of a fictitious group as an excuse to be away from her and their children. It didn't matter. She would get through this night and figure out how to handle her husband later.

As she walked toward her kitchen, she found an old broken hair dryer lying on the chair in her formal living room, "What the?" Dennis hardly had any hair left to speak of. One of the kids probably left it here for some strange reason. She picked it up, took it to the kitchen, and threw it in the trash.

Forty Six

Mario walked the short distance from the hospital to the Cathedral Metropolitano where his latest nightmare began. He had a strange feeling he missed something with regards to Father Salazar and he needed to go back to the source to find out.

He jogged up the stone steps out front and the image of Angela's lifeless body rushed back to him. He realized he would never enter the Cathedral again without thinking about her. His frustration and determination collided when he thought about how these evil maniacs ruined his family and now threatened to tear apart the church that served such an important role for the city. *I have to find you, Father Salazar. I will find you.*

Mario pushed on the heavy doors at the main entrance and walked inside, surprised to see the place completely empty. "Hello?" He walked through the sanctuary, stood between the pews and called out again. "Hello?"

He walked toward the back, fully expecting any of a handful of nuns or other clergy to come wandering out any minute, as they always did in the past, but still, nobody ever appeared. Mario thought back to the other night when he came to help the poor frightened choirboy. "Hello?" Still no answer.

Something wasn't quite right here, but he couldn't put his finger on it just yet. He walked back outside as the sun started going down. He needed to get back to his mother and see to it she and Sylvia got out of their respective homes tonight. He knew one thing for sure – nobody was safe.

***

Sister Hernandez heard the footsteps and the sound of the voice above her head. "In here."

All the nuns called out for help, but unfortunately, during the entire captivity, nobody upstairs could hear them down here in the crypt. In times past, the Archbishop's crypt was opened to the public, but that was years ago now, so the heavy doors barricading the space remained nearly impenetrable to sounds.

One nun pounded her fists against the door. "Oh no. Please don't leave us down here, help us."

"Sister." Sister Hernandez shushed. "Please calm yourself down. Keep faith and be patient. We have food to eat, shelter and the company of each other. There must be hope for us yet."

"But why haven't they come for us? Why hasn't anyone noticed we're missing? Surely someone must realize we're gone by now," another nun cried hysterically.

A cold chill ran through Sister Hernandez' heart when she realized at that moment, she and she alone, carried sole blame for the suffering of them all. If she had the courage to let her captor kill her on the spot the other night and told Mario Martinez about the others, he would have found Father Salazar still alive. She was selfish, and now they all suffered. "Someone will find us. They will figure it out," she reassured them. "Now please, calm yourselves down."

Sister Hernandez tried to hide the growing fear and mounding guilt in her own heart. She never realized they would be trapped in here so long or she might have been more courageous the other night, but now, it was too late. Her selfishness put them all in jeopardy, and rather than sacrificing herself for them all, they might all die in here together. If she ever got freed from this, she would require many confessions to rid her soul of these burdens.

The air down here was thin, and she herself started to feel dizzy from lack of proper ventilation. She realized without help, they would all soon drift to sleep and go off quietly to the hereafter and nobody would know about it. She prayed for justice for those tyrants who tortured them so, and she prayed to live long enough to help bring it around and right the wrongs she caused them all.

Forty Seven

Bella decided to park herself in front of the Palacio so she could be first on the scene if anything exciting happened out here tonight. With two murders in the past twenty four hours, tonight might bring even more big news stories.

She sat on a folding chair Pedro kept for her in the truck and filed her fingernails when she happened to see Mario walking down the steps over at the Cathedral. She got up and started running. "Hey Mario."

He stopped and stared at her with his arms crossed. "What do you want?"

"Did you see about getting me that interview with *El Presidente* yet?"

"Do you have any idea how stupid you are?" Mario growled. "Father Salazar was kidnapped from the hospital today after undergoing a serious surgery and now I can't find him and I have no leads. He might die because of you. So excuse me if I don't have time to get you any new stories tonight." Mario turned and ran off.

"But wait. I'm sorry. I didn't mean to."

"You should have called me, Bella. Now it might be too late."

***

Elsa and Sylvia cleaned up all the dishes by the time Mario arrived at the house shortly after dark. "Get your things together," he told them. "We're going to my house tonight."

"But Mario," his mother protested.

"No discussion, Mama. I'm not in the mood. Your window is torn out, Sylvia's place is a mess and you can't stay here. My team will come tomorrow to take care of this and see if we can find some clues, but meanwhile, I don't take no for an answer."

"I'll go next door and get my things," Sylvia told them.

"I'll check it out first to make sure it's safe. You two need to be ready in five minutes."

"I'm not done with the dishes, Mario," Elsa said.

"I don't care. Do it, please. I am worried about your safety." He kissed her on the cheek.

Elsa threw down her dishtowel and smiled. "You are a good son. I'll go get ready."

***

Mario walked up the hill toward his house from the metro station carrying all of his mother and Sylvia's belongings on his back. He paused at the bottom of the final incline to catch his breath ."What did you two bring? Both kitchen sinks and everything in the refrigerators?"

"We need to look our best," Elsa smiled.

"Si and we have to eat," Sylvia said.

Elsa nodded. "You're right, Sylvia. My son doesn't believe in keeping food in his house."

Mario rolled his eyes. "Alright."

Elsa smiled. "We nearly starved to death the last time we were here."

"Okay. I get the message. Next time I promise to buy some food, okay? Speaking of which…" The neighborhood lit up and he smelled food cooking on his neighbor's grill outside. "We're almost there now."

"You're right," Elsa said. "It does smell good. Mario, what should we do about dinner tonight?"

Up in the distance, he noticed something wasn't right. "Shhh."

"Don't shhhh me," Elsa complained.

"Quiet. I need to listen. Please stop a minute." He held his hand out to block them from going further. He scanned his front yard and did a double take. Surely this couldn't be…He could've sworn he saw huge concrete chunks on the ground by his front windows and in the street near his home. As he took a few steps closer, he got a sick feeling in his stomach. "You two wait right here."

"Mario, what are you doing?" Elsa asked.

He pulled his gun. "Stay off the street, over by those bushes, and wait until I come get you, comprende?" He dropped the knapsack with their belongings next to his mother.

His mother's eyes filled with fear. "What is it?"

"Something isn't right, Mama. I should have listened to Bene and got the two of you into a safe place right after the funeral today. Now I'm afraid it's too late."

Forty Eight

Montoya got in his car and drove downtown to the location for tonight's meeting. He parked around the corner from the Cerro de la Estrella and waited, munching down some tacos he picked up at a local drive through. He still found himself fuming over his run in with his wife earlier. He wanted to leave a little later, grab a light dinner at home, but his wife messed that up by becoming a meddling fool. She was so convinced he was out having an affair. It irked him. He fought her accusations for years before realizing it served as a perfect excuse for his late nights out, and missed family functions, so eventually he stopped trying to convince her otherwise.

He often wondered what she might think if she ever found out the truth. Would she be relieved he'd been faithful, or would she horrified? He tried telling her about his involvement with a religious organization, but she always argued, insisting he made up tall tales to avoid telling her about his mistress.

Montoya still laughed about that. He knew he didn't have much in the way of looks, and after being married this long, even if he thought he could attract women, he would hardly know how to handle anyone other than his wife.

As darkness settled around the city, Montoya finished eating and checked his watch -7:30p.m. He saw dozens of people parking and walking toward the hill, all wore regular street clothes, but Montoya knew why they were here. Within minutes from now, he would finally claim the title he always felt destined for, ever since joining this organization many years ago. Tonight, his destiny would unfold.

***

Father Salazar woke up in the dark in excruciating pain, "Help. Where am I?"

The man in the leather jacket glanced in the rearview mirror of his SUV, "Shut up old man or you'll be sorry."

Salazar cringed as the car tore around a corner. His incision burned and caused incredible pain. "Please young man, have mercy on me. You can still ask and be forgiven for what you've done here, I promise."

The car came to an abrupt halt. "Quiet." He climbed out of the car and opened the back door, held up a long needle and brought it toward the priest.

"Wait. Please no." As the drugs shot through Father Salazar's veins, he prayed for mercy while he drifted swiftly away from the waking world.

***

The man in the black leather jacket smiled as he watched hundreds of people descend on the Cerro de la Estrella, many of whom were captured earlier this afternoon in a raid of the government offices all over the city. By tomorrow morning, terror would spread like the new fires to all areas in Mexico City and the gods would be pleased.

For tonight, he would revel in the thrill of watching the church leadership crumble to the ground, vengeance from angry gods dethroned nearly five hundred years before.

He stood at the entrance to the area and watched the bound and gagged prisoners arriving at the new fire ceremony, along with offerings of new and used appliances ceremoniously dumped in the center of the circle. Soon it would all be set ablaze, and before the fire department could get wind of it, they would be long gone. Life in all its glory would become peaceful for the next fifty seven years, and soon, he would reach his personal goals and climb to heights he'd always dreamed of.

"What should we do with them?" someone asked about the prisoner he led into the area.

"Bring him in, keep his mouth gagged, but make sure he sees what's happening here, because soon, they will receive the same treatment."

"Yes, sir."

Off in the distance, the man saw the person he'd been waiting for. He stepped away from his post, met him in the parking lot, "Senor Montoya, so wonderful to see you."

Montoya scowled. "Shhhh. Nobody's supposed to know it's me." He donned his black ski mask and followed his host into the sacred area.

"Did you happen to bring your offering?"

Montoya gulped. "No, my wife stopped me. I forgot it, but I'm sure nobody will notice."

"You're probably right. No need for the new leader to bother bringing an offering to the gods." The man in the leather jacket smiled. This would be easier to pull off than he originally thought.

Forty Nine

By the time he reached his front yard, Mario nearly collapsed at the sight of it. The entire façade had been blown to smithereens by some type of automatic gunfire. He crunched through the rubble, kicking concrete out of his way so he could get to his door. He tried the doorknob which broke off in his hand, and walked into the living room, expecting to see a scene similar to his mother and Sylvia's houses. Surprisingly, other than the debris from the plaster and glass, it didn't look like anyone had been inside, although he did a quick inspection just to make sure. Once he made sure they were alone, he went back outside.

His mother and Sylvia stood next to his mailbox crying. "What are we going to do now, Mario?" Elsa asked her son.

"What we should have done a long time ago. I'm calling Bene and having you set up in a safe house until all this blows over."

Elsa pulled a tissue from her purse and blew her nose. She started to look around and walked to his mailbox, pulling a white paper off the door. She looked it over. Her hands trembled.

"What is it, Mama?" he said.

"This is for you." She held the paper out for him to read and began to cry.

***

Bella Perez ate a Quarter Pounder and sat on the sidewalk of the Plaza de la Constitucion in the same suit she'd worn all day, waiting and watching the Palacio just in case anything interesting happened. So far, things around here were run of the mill. More than likely, the excitement from the last two days was over.

"Aren't you ready to go homes yet?" Pedro asked her. "We've worked more than eight hours today, you know."

"No. Not yet. Eat your Big Mac and shut up. I've got a feeling there's a story to crack out here tonight and we will sit here until something shows up."

"I'm tired. My back hurts. I want to go."

Bella checked her watch. "Thirty more minutes. Give me thirty more and if nothing happens, we go. Okay?"

Pedro rolled his eyes, threw his arms in the air. "Whatever. I'll wait for you in the truck where it's safe. I don't want to get shot at."

Bella laughed and munched on her fries. She watched people wandering through the Zocalo. This was her night to shine, she knew it…

"Hey."

She turned around when she heard the sound of the young man's voice, thinking it was Pedro complaining again. "What do you want?"

A tall kid, probably around her age, with an unseasonably warm hoodie sweatshirt towered over her. "Here."

"What's this?"

He shrugged. "I don't know but I think you might want to watch it."

She looked down at the videotape, pulled it from the plastic sleeve to see if there were any markings on it, and when she looked up again, the kid was long gone. She crumpled her hamburger bag up in the trash and went to get back in the van.

***

Mario snapped the parchment paper from his mother's trembling hands and read it:

Mario Martinez
Warning
Cathedral Metropolitano
Nine tonight
Come alone or many will die.

Elsa sunk to her knees and sobbed, clutching his pant leg. "You can't go there tonight. Please. I buried one child today, I won't survive without you. Please don't go."

He took a deep breath and crushed the paper in his hands. "I have to do this. These people are not going to terrorize my family, kill my friends and think they can get away with it anymore. You will come with me, and once I get you settled someplace safe, I will go to this place and end these people once and for all."

"No." Elsa cried.

"She's right, Mario, it's too dangerous," Sylvia agreed.

"I have to do this. I refuse to live in fear. They've already taken everything from us and there is nothing to lose. I must stop them and I promise the two of you I will. Angela and Carlos did not die in vain."

"But you don't even know who you're fighting." Sylvia said.

"I am fighting the people who killed our family. That is enough. Come on, we've got to hurry."

***

Benito and Juarez Senior just finished their drinks and were about to call it a night when the phone rang. Bene listened intently to the situation. "Mario, I want you three to meet me downtown as soon as you can. Take the Metro. I believe you're safer there. Your mother and Sylvia will stay in the guest quarters in my father's house tonight, and as for you...I don't like this one bit..."

"Bene, my mother's already asked me not to go, but you know I have to, don't you? It's not about Angela anymore, or Salazar. We need to live in peace, and we can't rest until someone stops them."

"Si. I will make a call to our team of ten, see if they can..."

"They said nobody but me, Bene. If we're going to pull this off, I've got to go it alone."

"I never give in to terrorist demands, Mario, and I won't start now."

"I understand, but these people obviously mean business. They will not play with anyone but me. They're probably mad about what happened the other night when you got away. There is no other way to stop them. Besides, I still have my vest on, so I'll be fine."

Bene sighed. "The ten officers I assigned to you are all tactical experts. There are ways to carefully take these people out one by one..."

"Do I need to argue with you like I do with my mom, brother? Please. They're going to try and pull a stunt with Father Salazar tonight, and I don't want to do anything to put him or anyone else in jeopardy."

"But you saw what they did last time…"

"Si and I fought them alone in that also, up until the time the shooting started. Trust me Bene, please."

"I don't like it, but apparently I have no choice." Bene hung up the phone and reached for the scotch.

"What's wrong, son?" Juarez Senior asked.

"Father, Mario's in too deep. We need to pull all available resources tonight to help him."

Fifty

Montoya marched behind the throngs of nameless, faceless people who gathered at *Cello de la Estrella*. He took his rightful place front and center, next to the master of ceremonies, and waited for the event to begin.

"Gather around brothers and sisters." The man in the black leather jacket lifted his arms. "Tonight is a special evening, and let me show you why." He pulled on a rope and at the end of it, the terrorized Father Salazar trembled and stepped forward, "Tonight we will honor the gods, testing them to see if they are pleased or not, and we will honor them with one of the greatest sacrifices of all."

The crowd applauded and went wild at the sight of the priest.

"I trust each of you brought the household items and you placed those in the center of our circle tonight as part of our offering to our gods, yes?"

The crowd shouted their agreement. "Yes."

"Very good. We have another special guest tonight. This man here. His face is currently hidden, but soon we will reveal the one who has been chosen to replace our former *Huitzilopochtli* after his untimely demise the other night during our *Noche Triste* ceremony."

Mumbling erupted amongst the crowd.

"Quiet everyone. I trust you knew that your god was executed the other night, did you not?"

Montoya listened to the shocked reactions of the crowd. The bad feeling he had all day returned. He wasn't at all sure about the direction this ceremony was headed. He hated feeling fearful, especially since being elevated to priest status, but although it might displease the gods, he had a strange feeling he needed to run away and never look back.

"Yes, it's true," the man in leather continued, "The other night, *Huitzilopochtli* was murdered during the *Noche Triste* ceremony, but our other god, *Quetzalcoatl* was released and freed by an outsider. Now this man…" He pointed straight at the hooded Montoya. "…claims to be our new god, but he cannot possibly hold a position of such high regard when he does not even understand our customs. This man did not bring an offering of any kind to the gods tonight. For that reason, I believe he is the impostor, sent to destroy us all by our enemies. He must be sacrificed immediately before our gods become even more enraged than they already are."

Dennis felt dizzy from the sound of his death warrant and the mobs shouting and threatening to destroy him. "No," he said. "The Great One chose me."

"Impostor." The leather jacket man pulled Montoya's mask off and revealed his trembling identity to all who stood by watching. "Kill him. Kill him before he enacts revenge on us and destroys our entire civilization."

Dennis took off running straight into the crowd because the space was so compact he saw no place else to go. He knew the sacrificial instruments would be set up near the center of the crowd, and hoped if he ran through them, he could escape to his car amidst the confusion.

"Kill. Kill. Kill." Soon this erupted into a chant and the people pulled out their blades.

Dennis just reached the opening to the circle, about to step outside when he felt the piercing sting of obsidian slash through his gut. He slumped forward to the ground while the thug responsible stood triumphantly over him, laughing while the crowd cheered, chanted and clapped.

Once he fell to the ground bleeding, and all eyes turned back to the Master of Ceremonies who still shouted orders at the group, Dennis Montoya got up, clutched his stomach and ran for his life down the hill, all the while, praying to god he would make it home or to a hospital before it was too late.

Fifty One

Mario stood in Bene's office with his mother and Sylvia. He didn't like the idea of leaving the two of them anywhere, but he had no choice. "I am entrusting you with their lives."

Benito obviously sensed his concerns. "I give you my word the ladies will be safe. We are taking them to my father's house right now, where they will each have a private room and bath until this gets cleared up. There's room for you too…"

Mario rolled his eyes. "Later."

"I'll hold you to it." Bene pat him on the back. "I see you're wearing your vest…"

Mario chuckled. Benito sounded more like a big brother with each passing day. "Si, and my guns are locked and loaded."

Elsa ran and held him. "Promise you will come home safe, Mario, please."

He held Elsa's face in his hands, kissed her cheeks, "Mama, I'll be back to you in an hour or two. I must find Father Salazar."

"Be careful out there," Bene slapped Mario on the back before he turned to go.

Mario smiled and waved. "Hasta luego all of you. Say a prayer for me."

***

Father Salazar felt dizzy. He didn't quite know what just happened here, but he knew enough to realize someone probably just got murdered.

"Now we will take our special sacrifice to our sacred site for tonight – the tomb of the Archbishops under the Cathedral Metropolitano. Go safely. We will begin our ceremonies at nine sharp, during the hour of completion." He looked at his watch. "It is 8:30 now so go on, brothers and sisters. Let us light the fires and prepare to make our restitution to our gods." He stuck a match and threw it into the middle of the pit filled with beat up used electronics, bed linens, bathroom supplies. Soon everyone joined in and together they created an inferno. Smoke billowed into the night sky as the noxious fumes consumed everything.

Salazar wanted to run away, but the rope around his neck and arms and the fresh incision in his chest prevented him from doing much.

"Come on you. Now." the man dragged him through the crowd, pulling his collar like a bad dog until they reached the truck. He picked up Salazar and threw him against the floorboard. "Pretty soon you will meet your maker, Father." He laughed. "It will be quite a show too. I invited some very special guests to witness your exit from this life," he laughed, "In fact, I can't wait to see the looks on their faces when they see us slice you in two."

***

Bella was glad she finished her burger before viewing the video because otherwise she would have been sick.

The tape showed the party headquarters for each of the political parties in Mexico. The film showed clear shots of the signs outside the buildings and masked men who held the workers at gunpoint. They went inside offices of all the major figures, shouting and waving guns in their faces before gagging them and slipping black masks over their faces and roughhousing them in to a plain white van.

The video went on and on, and when one van filled, another showed up and it too eventually filled with people.

Finally, a note scrolled across the screen: *Want a big scoop, Bella Perez? Keep your big mouth shut and we'll be in touch.*

For the first time in her short life, Bella Perez felt at a loss for words. She looked over at Pedro. "What do you think?"

"I think this is pretty f'ed up, if you ask me."

She wanted something exciting and now realized to be careful what you wish for. "What are we gonna do?"

Pedro shrugged. "I dunno. I want to go home."

Bella remembered a half baked promise she made a friend earlier. "I have an idea."

Fifty Two

Mario arrived to the Cathedral Metropolitano at 8:59p.m, gun within reach, ready for whatever or whoever he might encounter inside. He crept up the steps and burst through the front door, gun drawn. "Hello?"

Strangely, like this afternoon, nobody was anywhere in sight. He kept his gun extended in front of him, walking through the church, peeking around the golden altars and into the many side chapels, waiting for something to happen, or someone to jump out at him. Still nothing. There were no sounds, no pleas for help, and certainly nothing going on in here even remotely similar to what happened the night of July 1st, when Benito nearly lost his life.

He stepped carefully toward the back of the sanctuary, past the confessionals, toward the door leading out to the alley where so much bloodshed occurred earlier. "Hello? Is anybody there?"

Suddenly in the stillness, a shrill scream broke the silence. Mario spun around, wondering where it came from, until he heard it again, this time louder than before. Then he realized what he failed to see all along - *the sound is coming from underneath the floor.*
***

Dennis Montoya was no fool. He realized he would most likely not make it to see the sunrise. The hospital was twice as far from *Cerro de la Estrella* as his house, so rather than running completely out of time, if he could redeem his sinful soul, he should go home, face his wife, tell her the truth, and not go to the grave having her wonder about his fidelity. She deserved more, but at least he could offer that much.

He pulled up the driveway of his high end home, stumbling and bleeding all over the sidewalk, until he reached the front door and knocked. He fumbled with his keys. His head spun from too much blood and he feared he would pass out.

The porch light clicked on, and when his wife opened the door, he fell on their steps.

She ran to him, knelt down and screamed. "Dennis."

"Please," he whispered. "Mario Martinez…tell him…*El Templo*…" Although he wanted to tell his wife so much more, with that final proclamation, Dennis Montoya breathed his last. As he floated out of this life, the last thing he heard was the sound of his wife's bitter tears.
***

Right at nine o'clock sharp, ten of the Presidential Elite prescreened guards surrounded Cathedral Metropolitano, each wearing pure black latex and protective body armor from head to toe.

Despite Mario's wishes to keep matters private, Bene knew he needed backup, so he made the call. He could never live with himself if anything happened to him. Once there were any signs of struggle from inside, the team would descend on the church and assist in making arrests and putting an end to this mess once and for all.

The men waited outside, but never heard a word. One radioed to another, "Hey, do you think this is a trap? A bomb? Or do you think they might be set up someplace else?"

The other, who hid in the bushes on the side of the building near the Tabernacle entrance radioed back. "I don't know, but something's definitely wrong."

When the sounds of gunfire ripped through the night, the team leader gave the cue. "We're going in, boys."

Fifty Three

"I am pleased you all are here tonight for our official sacrifice to our gods here in the Archbishops Crypt. Welcome brothers and....*sisters*. Bring the Sisters in."

Frac stood in the back and watched the entire group of nuns march toward the altar. Even though he believed in the old ways, he had a sick feeling about this. He grew up Catholic and it didn't seem right to torture anyone who dedicated his or her life to God.

The Sisters filed in one by one, silent for the most part, other than a few who cried and sniffled.   One younger sister burst into fits of hysteria when she saw Father Salazar. He looked terrible and could barely stand on his own.

"Father. Father." the nun cried out to him and one of her captors swiftly slapped her to the ground.

The man in black leather continued. "Our gods demand blood sacrifice and tonight we will give it to them."

They tossed the priest down on a stone crypt belonging to Juan de Zumarraga, Mexico's first Archbishop. "You will die Salazar, right here, on the tomb of your ancestor." He ripped the priest's clothes open, shocked by what he saw there.

Salazar's chest had already been torn open the previous day by the heart surgeons who saved his life. Thick metal staples held his body together, and for a brief moment, the leathered leader hesitated, apparently stunned by the gore of the surgical injury.

Frac wasn't quite sure why he stopped and lowered his obsidian blade, but he felt relieved.

The crowd gasped.

"Our gift to the gods is tainted," the man in the black leather jacket announced. "We must resort to the next most suitable offering." He turned to the nuns and grabbed Sister Hernandez by the collar and dragged her toward him.

The other nuns screamed out in horror.

"Stop." A man with a gun burst through the door. "Hold it right there. Put her down, now!"

***

Mario pointed the gun at the crazy man in the leather jacket. He would have dropped him right there and then had it not been for the close proximity of all the Sisters and Father Salazar on the altar.

For some strange reason, the man looked slightly dazed. He released Sister Hernandez and she toppled to the floor. Once he took a half an inch step back, Mario shot him straight through the heart. He fell forward on to Salazar, probably injuring the poor priest.

"Everybody get out of here or you're next." He waved his gun in the air at the hoards of hooded men who filled the cathedral. He wished they could apprehend them all now, send them all the prison, but with such a small team in place, there would be no way to end this all tonight.

Mario ran up to help Father Salazar, while the hooded congregation started to take off, running for their lives out the exits.

The nuns rushed up to poor Father Salazar.

"Thank God you arrived." Sister Hernandez told Mario. "I've prayed you would find us ever since that first night."

Mario felt terrible for not finding them sooner, or even realizing they were missing. "I'm so sorry I didn't see it before, Sister. I should have known you were in duress. You acted so…"

Sister Hernandez clasped her hands in prayer. "You came. That's all that matters now. Our prayers were answered, thank you."

"It will be okay now." Mario kicked the leather man's lifeless body to the ground and leaned down to check on the old priest. Father Salazar looked worn out, but not fatal. He must be in his eighties by now, and with proper care, Mario figured he would survive this ordeal. "Father?" He whispered into the old man's ear.

Salazar opened his eyes and reached up to touch Mario's cheeks. "God bless you."

Mario remembered the first time he met Salazar the day Benito was kidnapped. So much happened since then. He would need to take Confession soon. "Lay still, Father. It will be alright. I'll call for help, and we will get you back to the hospital where you belong, okay?"

Just then the doors burst open and when Mario turned around, his team stood in the door, guns drawn, waiting to assist. He smiled. "I thought you'd never get here. Call an ambulance."

***

"Over the past five days, the man standing beside me saved hundreds of lives with his bravery, including my own. There are no words to describe my gratitude. He is a hero to his country, his fellow citizens and this city." Benito stood atop a stage next to a podium in the center of the Zocalo, right in front of Cathedral Metropolitano. "And so citizens of Mexico City, it is with great pride I present this Medal of Honor to Mario Martinez for acts of bravery to country and state." Benito hung a gold medallion on a green yellow red and white ribbon around his neck while the gathered crowd broke into thunderous applause.

Mario looked out and saw his mother and Sylvia in the front row. They were the only people who mattered now. Them and Benito. God he missed Angela. After all this, it would be tough to put the pieces of their lives back together, but even though he lost a sister, he found a brother in Bene. God gives and He takes away. He would try and forgive and find peace about what happened, hoping he could one day see it as part of some bigger plan. For now, the pain was still too raw. Just thinking about Angela made his eyes fill with tears. He stared down at the stage, not wanting to get caught crying. Plus, it was tough looking into such a huge crowd, embarrassing even. When Benito was the center of attention, that was fine, but Mario wasn't sure he enjoyed the limelight.

Benito turned to him and gave him a hug. "Great job."

"I didn't do anything," Mario whispered in his ear.

"Of course you did, you saved hundreds of lives."

"Yeah but I never knew about the nuns. I never even thought to look," Mario lowered his eyes in shame. "Plus we still need to get all the lab tests back…Those maniacs are still out there somewhere.

Bene sighed. "We're making progress."

Mario shrugged. "Still, I abandoned the nuns, Bene. My God!"

Benito laughed. "You're young, Mario. Just think of what you can do a few years from now. That's what I'm looking forward to."

Mario heard the sound of camera's clicking and saw a bright flash of tangerine in his side vision.

Bella Perez pushed her way to the front of the mob, shoved the microphone in his face. "How does it feel to be a hero, Mario?"

He shrugged and a slight smile crossed his lips. "Okay I guess."

Bella turned to face her camera and adoring fans. "There you have it Mexico City. Mario Martinez saves the Presidente and the beloved priest, Father Salazar who we are told is resting comfortably tonight thanks to one man's bravery. I'm Bella Perez reporting."

***

Ayala turned his TV off, took his feet off the desk and lit a cigar. For now, things were okay. Today, he was still safe. He would wait and see what tomorrow would bring...

The End

About the Author

Annette Shelley is a lifelong sci-fi and horror fan

and author of several novels and short stories.

She loves living in the worlds she creates.

Visit Annette online:

www.annetteshelley.com